A PIECE OF JUSTICE

Books by Jill Paton Walsh

A PIECE OF JUSTICE

An Imogen Quy Mystery

Jill Paton Walsh

St. Martin's Press
New York

Library of Congress Cataloging-in-Publication Data

Paton Walsh, Jill
A piece of justice : an Imogen Quy mystery / Jill Paton Walsh.
p.   cm.
ISBN 0-312-29252-X
I. Title.
PR6066.A84P54   1995
823'.914—dc20   95-2823   CIP

First published in Great Britain by Hodder & Stoughton

First U.S. Edition: August 1995

10 9 8 7 6 5 4 3 2 1

For R.H., a true original

This equal piece of justice – death . . .
Sir Thomas Browne

A PIECE OF JUSTICE

I

'Where's the repeat?' asked Imogen Quy. She was sitting surrounded by scraps of fabric, patterned and plain in a rainbow of colours, spread all over the floor. Pansy Whitman and Shirl Nichols were sitting in her armchairs, and the three of them were passing the pattern book to and fro. They were a quorum of the Newnham Quilters' Club, setting out to make a quilt to be raffled just before Christmas for the Red Cross funds. A little pleasant disagreement was afoot. Shirl wanted an elaborate pattern, involving piecing curves; Pansy wanted bright colours and easy shapes. Both of Imogen's friends liked quilts made with different blocks, put together on a grid with plain borders separating one from the next. Imogen liked patterns that overspilled, running across the entire surface of the work. There were many patterns like this; one block merged with the next, so that the patterns shifted as you looked, part of one block completing squares or diamonds in the next. They had lovely traditional names: 'Lost Sail', 'Compass Rose', 'Drunkard's Path', 'Delectable Mountains', 'Blazing Star', 'Homeward Bound', 'Barn-raising' . . .

Shirl was suggesting one called 'Pumpkin Patch', all curved seams. Pansy was pointing out how easy to sew was a pattern called 'Birds in the Air'.

'So boring, Pansy,' Shirl said.

'Not if we make it in lovely colours,' said Pansy.

'It's supposed to be special,' said Shirl. 'It won't raise lots of money if everyone thinks they could jolly well make it themselves.'

'They won't think that, whatever else,' said Pansy. 'People can't sew these days. They're all too busy taking doctorates and working in the City. They can't so much as darn a sock. And as for cooking – putting ready-meals in the microwave is too much for some I know!'

'Nearly everyone in the Quilters' Club is ancient!' said Shirl, agreeing. 'The whole art will die out soon.'

'Craft,' said Pansy.

'What?'

'It's a craft, not an art.'

'Oh, Pansy, don't!' said Shirl. 'Such a cop-out. Why isn't it an art? Just because women do it?'

'No,' said Pansy. 'That is . . . well . . .'

'What do you think, Imogen?' said Shirl.

'Sorry,' said Imogen. 'I wasn't listening, I'm afraid. I was trying to find the repeat in this one.' She showed them a page of the pattern book. It was covered with outlines of patchwork patterns – elaborate networks of lines, making a mesh of shapes all over the page. Somewhere in the mesh was an area that repeated; that was the block. You made however many blocks were required for the size of the proposed quilt, and sewed them together. Once sewn together they made patterns larger than themselves, which flowed in and out of adjacent blocks, danced and dazzled and pleased the eye.

The pattern Imogen was studying was called 'Coast o' Maine'. It had a flowing curved wavy look to it, although it was made only of triangles and squares.

'Here,' said Shirl, running a pencil line round an area of the diagram. The moment she isolated a square of the mesh Imogen could see how the whole page was made just of this pattern, repeated. The second row was offset by half a block, making it harder to see.

'Hey, that's nice!' said Pansy, looking over her shoulder. 'What about making that one?'

'I'll go along with that,' said Shirl. The pattern looked much harder to piece than it was; it seemed to have curves running through it. Shirl couldn't bear to be seen doing anything easy.

'Right,' said Imogen. 'Colours next. You start, I'll make some coffee.'

Choosing fabrics for the blocks was an intriguing process. Every time she did it Imogen started out picking up tastefully blending scraps, in soft harmonising colours. The three friends wielded scissors, cutting sample shapes, and laying them together to see what the stitched block would look like. The carefully chosen prints and plains in gentle harmony always looked dull. Pretty, and boring. The fact was, patchwork was a folk art – it didn't like being used in good taste – ghastly good taste was the expression that came to mind. Pansy might be lazy about sewing curved seams, but she had a wonderful eye for colours – clashing, unlikely colours that talked to each other across the grid of shapes, that looked bright and accidental. That wonderful 'found' look of old quilts, that Imogen loved, that spoke of need, and thrift, and using what you had to hand, the very absolute opposite of going into Laura Ashley and buying bits specially cut up and chosen to tone with each other, needed some daring to imitate. Reaching over Imogen's pleasant, ordinary looking choice of colours, Pansy tried a square of orange cloth, printed in scarlet blotches, alongside the dark red central star, removing the lilac that had been Imogen's first guess.

'Hmm,' she said, tilting her head. 'No . . . perhaps . . .' She swapped one of the soft blues for a bright turquoise, completely out of key with the other colours. It looked lovely. They sipped their coffee, and contemplated the result. Before the two friends left, they had worked out a yardage for a big double quilt, and cut out the templates from thick art-shop card. Next week they would cut out the fabric, sort it and distribute it to the members of the Quilters' Club for sewing into blocks. Imogen was always surprised at the large number of club members who liked to be given the block worked out, and cut out. All they had to do was the sewing. The fun of choosing and designing had all been greedily gobbled up by Shirl and Pansy and herself. Of course, anyone who wanted to could come to the planning session; the others must really truly prefer just to sew. And they were a good lot; kindly, unassuming, hard-working women, ready to make jam, or sew for any good cause; to arrange flowers in churches, to shop for neighbours, to baby-sit, to feed cats for absent friends. Salt of the earth sort of people. Heads down sort of people, reluctant to take credit.

Here in this modest little suburban corner, within easy walk of the centre of Cambridge the contrast, Imogen reflected, was not so much between housewives and women with doctorates – half the housewives *were* women with doctorates. It was a question of how people saw what they did. Of what counted for credit, so to speak. And one way or another, simple skills – domestic skills, the ability to make comfortable beds, and arrange rooms pleasantly, to preserve fruits in season, and make the little back gardens grow flowers and tomatoes and beans, to bring roast beef to table perfectly done at the same moment as perfectly done roast potatoes and Yorkshire pudding: all these abilities were disregarded; taken for granted by those who had them, not thought of as achievements worth crediting oneself with. Not taking credit for the altogether more arcane skills required for the quilt was part of the culture. Best not even call it an art. 'Craft' was more like it, Imogen reflected, in more ways than one.

Imogen settled in her breakfast room, with her sandwich lunch, and the newspaper propped on the water-jug to keep her company.

3

She didn't need to go in to work that day, because the college didn't need her much during the long vacation; it was in the short hectic terms – the Michaelmas term began next week – that college nurses like Imogen were worked off their feet. The newspaper was supposed to help Imogen not worry by keeping her mind off Frances Bullion, her lodger. Not that it was up to Imogen to worry about Fran; she was not a relative, and she had a mother of her own in the Midlands somewhere, whose duty it was, one supposed, to provide all the necessary worry about Fran. Imogen wasn't old enough to worry about Fran; Fran must be twenty-two or so, and Imogen was only a dozen years older. But Imogen, whose own life had been sidetracked by a disastrous love affair some years back, and who would have had children of her own by now if life had gone according to plan, had plenty of unused affection locked away carefully, and Fran had somehow come in for a share of it. Entitled or not, Imogen just did worry about Fran. Nothing in the newspaper was nearly interesting enough to stop her.

Making coffee she confronted the worry head on. Frances so desperately wanted to be an academic. What Cambridge ineffably called a 'don'. She had got to know Imogen as an undergraduate at St Agatha's, where Imogen worked as college nurse, and although the little flat in the top of Imogen's comfortable house in Newnham was not usually let to someone from St Agatha's, Imogen had happily made an exception for Fran when she stayed on at Cambridge doing postgraduate work. In one way things fell out luckily for Fran. She was interested in the relationship between biography and autobiography, as the subject for her dissertation. And Cambridge had just established a new chair in Biography – the History Faculty had refused to have anything to do with it, and it was under the aegis of the English Faculty – and Professor Maverack, the appointed first incumbent, had agreed to supervise Frances. The problem was money. Fran didn't have any.

She had, of course, a minimal grant. It left her short of nearly everything. Imogen couldn't afford to do without the rent, even if Fran would have accepted that. She had, without Fran's knowledge, lowered it somewhat – she had wanted Fran as a tenant, wanted for once someone that she liked, whose company would be an advantage. She did her best to feed Fran, giving her dinner several times a week, while still trying *not* to feed the two undergraduates from Clare College who rented her two spare

4

bedrooms, and whose unauthorised raids on the refrigerator made catering difficult.

A helpful professor would find teaching for his graduate students, to organise some earning power for them. But the Biography chair was new, Professor Maverack was new. He hadn't developed a network of contacts yet. Frances had struggled through the previous term without any earning power except doing a night duty on the petrol pumps at the garage on the Barton Road. This morning she had gone to see Professor Maverack to tell him that she didn't think she could continue indefinitely without some kind of teaching work. This interview would be complicated by the fact that Fran didn't like Professor Maverack. She hadn't told Imogen that, Imogen just knew. And Imogen was afraid she would draw a blank, and decide to throw it all up and get a job in an office somewhere. Imogen's own chance at getting qualified as a doctor had slipped through her fingers, and that made it much more painful for her to contemplate the same sort of thing happening to someone she cared for.

Not that Josh – the nearest thing Fran had to what used to be called a boyfriend – was anything like the sort of danger that Imogen's lover had been to her. Far from telling Fran to abandon her career, and devote herself to looking after him, Josh was given to putting his feet up on the fender, swinging back in the battered armchair, and hoping Fran would cut out a dazzling path of public achievement, and be able to support him while he minded the babies. Neither his own PhD nor Fran's seemed likely to come unstuck because of him. Imogen liked Josh.

She had abandoned the newspaper, with its thrilling headlines about glass panes falling out of the History Building, and had returned to contemplation of the patchwork block to try to stop worrying over the whole Frances saga yet again, when the front door slammed behind someone, and Frances herself called, 'Yoohoo! Imogen!' from the hall.

How seldom is worrying about someone justified! Fran came bouncing in, dropped her bag of notebooks on the floor, and collapsed in the armchair in Imogen's breakfast room, smiling happily.

'It's all right,' she said. 'He's got something for me.'

'Wonderful,' said Imogen. 'Terrific, Fran! What is it?'

'A little spot of ghosting,' said Fran. 'Quite well paid. Do you think I can do it? Whoo, hoo, haunt, haunt . . .'

'Fool,' said Imogen fondly. 'Now have a mug of coffee and tell me about it.'

'Well,' Fran began, turning on Imogen that clear-sighted, grey-eyed gaze of dauntless candour of which the owner was presumably unaware, 'there's this publisher who's after him. And he's far too busy himself. But he doesn't want to turn him down in case he's useful later . . .'

'Stop!' said Imogen. 'Slow down. Start again.'

Fran began her tale again. The gist of it was that there was a publisher – a well-known one, Recktype and Diss, who had approached Professor Maverack to complete a biography for them. They were desperate for it; it was already announced in their autumn catalogue and they needed it by August next year at the latest. They would pay a large advance. Maverack himself was too busy to do it in the time – he was working on his inaugural lecture, and had research of his own in progress. On the other hand the goodwill of Recktype and Diss was not to be sniffed at; scholarly biographies did not sell like hot cakes exactly, and Maverack could see himself approaching them to publish work of his own sooner or later. He would like to oblige them if he could. All the materials for the project had been assembled by an author who was unable to complete it. So the Professor proposed that Fran should write the book – it might even be useful for her in her own dissertation actually to have written a biography herself – and he would look it over and put his name to it. Of course, every penny of the advance would be Fran's. End of money problems. Everyone happy.

'But Fran, if you are going to write it, shouldn't your name be on the title page?' asked Imogen.

'Recktype and Diss wouldn't have it. They want a famous name on it, or it wouldn't sell at all. Wouldn't get serious reviews. He's promised to put my name on it somewhere – share the credit. Frankly, Imogen, getting a share of the credit for a project with his name on it won't do me any harm at all.'

'And in return for doing all the work . . .'

'I get all the money.'

'You didn't say who this biography is of?'

'Gideon Summerfield. He's a mathematician of some kind. He's about to get the Waymark Prize.'

'I've heard of Gideon Summerfield,' said Imogen.

'Clever you. That's more than I had.'

6

'He used to be a tutor at St Agatha's. Retired before you came up. He's dead now, surely.'

'The prize is posthumous.'

'But the biography is urgent?'

'The publishers expect the announcement of the prize to stir some interest. They had it all organised; started in good time. They put it in their catalogue. Someone called Mark Zephyr was doing it for them.'

'I get the picture,' said Imogen. 'You do this for them. It solves problems. It pays well, it puts you in the professor's good books . . .'

'I'm taking you out to dinner to celebrate,' said Fran happily. 'Let's go to that nice pub at Sutton Gault. But I must fly now, there's a lecture I want to hear.' She jumped up, and gathered up her books and notebooks. 'If a large box arrives for me, it will be the papers from Mark Zephyr. It's coming from the publisher's office by courier.'

As she left, Imogen called after her, 'Fran, why didn't Mark Zephyr finish the job?'

'He died,' yelled Fran from the front door, letting it slam behind her.

2

Urgency in the editorial department of Recktype and Diss did not translate very easily into urgency in the post-room, and it was three days before the papers for Fran's great project arrived. Imogen was cycling home when she saw the van blocking the narrow roadway between the parked cars, outside her own front door. She put on speed, and dismounted with a screech of brakes, just as the driver had given up knocking and waiting, and was about to drive off again. Imogen unlocked her front door, and he staggered up the path with a very large box, in a very battered state. It was bound up with string, and coming apart at all four corners, and clearly from his manner of carrying it very heavy. When Imogen asked him if he could possibly take it upstairs, he mentioned his heart. Imogen sympathised, and offered some beer money, whereupon the driver took several steps towards the stairs. Imogen wondered whether to tell him now, or when he reached the upstairs landing, that the destination of the box was the top flat, but before he had heaved himself and his burden more than three steps up from the hall, the box disintegrated.

String snapped, corrugated cardboard tore open, and bundles and sheets of paper thumped and fluttered everywhere. The driver cursed, and began to seize the fallen stuff, and thrust it back through the holes in the package. Imogen stopped him – Lord knows what confusion and destruction he was wreaking – and gave him some beer money anyway. Then she closed the door on him, made some coffee, and began to try to sort out the confusion herself.

It wasn't easy. Imogen pulled out the leaves of her dining-room table, to have room to spread things out. There was a stack of four stout box files labelled 'From Mark Zephyr'. Imogen put these unopened at one end of the table. Then there was a brown box, the kind of box dresses used to be packed in in smart shops, flattened at all four corners, but roughly intact. Imogen put that down beside the files, and turned her attention to the masses of papers that had

9

been loose in the outer box, and were now piled inside it, and lying widely scattered on her stairs and hall floor. It was quite difficult to sort out things when you didn't know what there was, or what order it ought to be in. Imogen contemplated simply leaving it all for Fran to handle; but she had someone coming to dinner that evening, and the table might well be wanted before Fran got in. No, better sort it roughly and carry it upstairs in parts to Fran's eyrie.

But what was supposed to be here? She found a torn and exploded wrapper marked – it took a bit of finding, for the thing was torn across the label – 'Return to JS'. Then there was an ancient paper file that had worn through and dumped out its contents from the back. That was labelled, in a different hand, a small neat one, 'Recovered from premises of May Swann'. Imogen inspected the loose papers. There were dozens of letters from many different correspondents, a desk diary from 1963, wallets of holiday snapshots, a list of Christmas card recipients . . . and a number of handwritten pages, closely covered in a clear handwriting, from a lined loose-leaf block. Guessing, Imogen put the random assortment of papers into a pile with the 'Return to JS' wrapper, and the manuscript pages into the May Swann file, which she repaired with parcel tape. Then she trudged up and down the two flights of stairs and laid the stuff out on Fran's little square table in the upstairs flat. She gazed around with some satisfaction – Fran was the first tenant Imogen had ever had who kept the place clean.

Now to remove the shattered ruins of the outer box, and the snarls of snapped string from the hall, and she could get on with her cooking – it was high time, all that had taken ages. As Imogen bent the box, and trod it flat to compact it enough to put it out by the dustbins, she saw a paper caught in the split angle, where the stupid driver had tried to thrust stuff back into the box. She extracted it. It was a sheet of office memo paper, with Recktype and Diss's monogram on the top. It said, 'Send at once, to Frances Bullion, address below, Zephyr files on Summerfield. *Keep back the rest.* M. Drawl.'

From the look of it, Imogen concluded, the despatch department had made a mistake, and sent off both the stuff they were supposed to keep and the instruction to keep it. Perhaps some of it wasn't about Summerfield, and Fran wouldn't have so much to deal with. But Imogen was in a hurry now; she propped the note behind the coffee jar on the kitchen dresser, and turned her mind to her cooking.

Imogen's dinner guest was Dr Malcolm Mistral, a fellow of St Agatha's. He was a widower, who had returned to live in college after many years in a handsome house in Newton Road. He had confessed to Imogen ruefully how he missed having quiet suppers at home with his wife – the wide open spaces of high table in the College Hall and the compulsory random company of college fellows and their guests discomforted him.

'Why not cook yourself supper in your rooms, now and then?' Imogen had asked. 'You've got a little kitchen haven't you?'

Malcolm Mistral had confessed to being unable to boil an egg. His wife hadn't let him so much as pick up a wooden spoon, all his long married life.

Imogen had taken to having him for a meal at home with her now and then. He often asked her for the recipe for whatever food she had served him, and she gave it to him carefully written out with full instructions; tactfully she never asked him if he had tried the recipes, or how he had got along with them. He invariably remarked that being male, and a college fellow, was not an absolute bar to being a good cook; Meredith Bagadeuce was an excellent cook. The only complaint against him on that head was that he didn't invite Malcolm Mistral very often.

Under cover of this supposed tutorial process Imogen had gradually got to know Dr Mistral. The thought that very clever people can sometimes make very dull company was one which Imogen kept firmly suppressed. Now, over coffee at her fireside in one of the long pauses that fell naturally into her conversation with someone with whom she had so little in common, it occurred to her to ask him if he had known Gideon Summerfield.

'Somewhat,' said Mistral. 'He was a research fellow when I first came to St Agatha's. Quite a bit younger than me. Saw him around though, of course. On a college committee with him once or twice. That sort of thing.'

'What was he like?' asked Imogen.

'I don't know, really. Decent sort of chap, I suppose. Worked hard for the college. Why do you ask?'

'A friend of mine has been asked to write his biography.'

'Really? You rather surprise me. Was he interesting?'

'That's what I was asking you!' said Imogen, laughing. 'Have a chocolate with a second cup of coffee, won't you?'

'You spoil me, Miss Quy,' he said, delicately picking a mint from the box.

Imogen wondered whether to ask him to call her Imogen, and then decided that she didn't feel quite ready to call him Malcolm; so she left it.

'I wouldn't have thought old Summerfield was worth a book,' he said, thoughtfully, 'though it's quite possible to be in the same college as someone for years and years and never know the least thing about them *privately*, you know. They could be wife-beaters or womanisers, or tricksters, or fraudsters, and their fellow fellows wouldn't realise a thing. We know each other very well on a narrow ambit. Wouldn't be surprised if *you* know more about us than we do about each other, d'you see?'

'Well, the healthier a fellow is the less I would know about him, as a rule,' said Imogen. 'But that narrow ambit on which you know each other well might have given you some sidelight on Gideon Summerfield?'

'As I say, I can't think of anything interesting about him. Why does anyone want a biography? Apart from Janet, that is?'

'Janet?'

'His wife. Widow, I mean. Fiercely devoted sort of woman. My wife – my late wife – knew her somewhat. She would want a biography if it confined itself strictly to praise. Devoted her life to the great man. That sort of woman. But I can't think who would actually want to *read* it . . .'

'I think he's about to get the Waymark Prize.'

'Yes; I heard that too. Might be true, I suppose.'

'But you would be surprised?'

'Of course, he was a mathematician,' said Malcolm Mistral, thoughtfully, taking another mint.

'Well, the Waymark Prize is specially for mathematics, isn't it?' asked Imogen.

'Yes, yes. But I meant merely, talent in mathematicians can be difficult to detect. For non-mathematicians, I mean.'

'You thought he wasn't clever?' said Imogen, joyfully egging her guest on.

'My dear Miss Quy, *every* fellow of St Agatha's is clever,' said Dr Mistral, sounding pained. 'The question is, was he brilliant? So brilliant that he merits the Waymark Prize? As you know, rather oddly there isn't a Nobel Prize for Mathematics, and the Waymark is supposed to make up for that. So to get that is to rate with Nobel Prize winners.'

'And you didn't think . . .?' Imogen felt unscrupulous to press on in this way, but she had cooked a very good dinner, and she was still hoping for a titbit for Fran, as quid pro quo.

'I believe he puzzled other mathematicians, too,' said Dr Mistral slyly. 'Of course, we don't understand each other's subjects. We can't estimate the worth of work in physics or history or law unless we are physicists or historians or lawyers. But you know in most cases you can feel yourself in the presence of a fine mind, even just talking commonplaces at high table. But Summerfield . . . well, some of his colleagues were surprised at what he had done. He was a perfectly respectable mathematician, but he didn't strike people as brilliant. Then he produced this one splendid piece of work, rather late in life, and then that was it. As I say he wasn't scintillating. I sat next to him once at a college feast and all he talked about all evening was that the Filet de Boeuf Wellington was tough.'

'His work was done late in life?'

'I only mean late for a mathematician.'

'They burn out early?'

'Not necessarily, I understand. But they usually start to be good very young – then they can keep it up for a long time. But to get much better in midstream is unusual. So Bagadeuce told me, and I suppose he would know.' Dr Bagadeuce was St Agatha's Director of Studies in Mathematics.

'He was rather odd, I thought,' continued Dr Mistral, 'about the rumour – the rumour that Gideon Summerfield was in the running for the Waymark, I mean. Very cool about it. Very cool. Considering how hot he usually is for the glory of the college.' He visited a malicious grin on Imogen. 'Can't have liked the fellow much, *I* thought.'

Imogen offered a choice of brandy or Cointreau to complete the evening.

As Dr Mistral was sipping his brandy and talking of leaving she asked, 'What was that one splendid piece of work that propelled Summerfield to fame? Do you know?'

'You're asking the wrong man, I'm afraid. Don't know a thing about maths. It was some kind of geometry, I think. Your friend should be able to ask Bagadeuce about it; he was very excited about it when it was first published.'

'Thank you,' said Imogen. 'I'll suggest it to her.'

'Her?'

'Her,' said Imogen, firmly. He had given himself away, expecting that a biographer would be male. But then he was a harmless enough sort of man, and of an earlier generation. The world had changed a good deal since his unconscious expectations had been formed. Perhaps, she thought, as she closed the door behind him – he never stayed late – she should not pamper him, but should give him recipes and leave him to it. On the other hand, what harm did it do to cook for him now and then? And tonight he had been useful in a way.

Only in a way; it didn't seem likely to be helpful to tell Fran what an old bore she was going to have to write about. An old bore with an adoring wife. Oh dear. She hadn't heard Fran come in, so she sat up for a while, waiting for her. She lit the gas logs that made such a pretty phoney fire in the Victorian grate in her front room, got out the piece bag, and the squared paper on which 'Coast o' Maine' had been drawn out, and began playing with swathes of cloth – patterned and plain in a rainbow palette of colours, cutting bits roughly to shape and laying them out to see what they looked like. The colour choices made earlier, when Shirl and Pansy were with her, were good, but there was no harm in trying to improve them.

The piece bag was slightly dangerous to Imogen. It put her in mind of the past. Here was a piece of finely striped shirting from the uniform of a trainee nurse; Imogen had once, some time ago, owned three of those, and worked very hard in them. Here, from longer ago still, was a lovely flower print on silk from which she had made herself a ball-gown to go to a Commemoration Ball at Oxford, while she was a medical student there, before she threw it all up to go to America with Frank. How different her life would have been if he hadn't suddenly dumped her in favour of another woman! Imogen put the scissors into the the folds of silk, and cut a sample diamond from it. Once this whole line of thought would have been horribly painful to her – now, she realised, she was on the whole grateful to have had her life as it was, instead of as it might have been. Frank was a trimmer, and sooner or later would have found a wind favourable to his plans, and left Imogen. She was probably lucky he had done it sooner rather than later. She had managed; she had come home, trained as a nurse, looked after her parents, found a niche in St Agatha's College, where she was appreciated. Most of the time, anyway. It was a job with some unlooked for perks – like friendship with Lady Buckmote, the Master's wife, known to one and all as Lady

B., a kind, sensible woman with a nice dry wit. She had made common cause with Imogen several times, and they were now fast friends.

The scrap of silk looked lovely in the patchwork square – was there enough to be useful? It had been bold of Imogen to buy anything so bright to wear with her very red hair. She stood up and held the silk in front of herself as she stared in the mirror above the mantelshelf. Her round, full, slightly freckled face looked back at her, framed in her carroty curls, above the dazzling orange and gold and pink of the print. A wonderful effect for a happy young woman going dancing with her lover – Imogen would never dare it now. 'Plain grey Alpaca for me, now,' she murmured, smiling at herself. It was late, and she was tired. Goodness knows how late Fran would come in – it might be any time until dawn when the young whooped it up with their friends. Imogen gathered the scraps into the bag, put out the lights, and went to bed. Talk about Summerfield would have to wait till morning.

3

'You wouldn't have some time to help me, would you?' Fran asked. It was a crisp fine Sunday morning, and Imogen had been intending a long walk. But it could wait for an hour. She trudged upstairs with Fran.

'I'll make coffee,' said Fran. 'This could be a big deal.'

Imogen took in the state of the little flat. Every flat surface – the seat of the settee, the expanse of the hearth rug, the dining table, the seat of every chair, was covered in papers. Piles of papers, files, bundles of letters, of index cards, of manuscript, typescript . . . There was nowhere to sit down.

'What can I do, exactly?' Imogen asked.

'Well, chiefly, I was hoping you might remember where some of this stuff fell apart from,' said Fran.

'Not a chance,' said Imogen cheerfully. 'It just exploded everywhere out of the box. I might be able to reconstruct my reconstruction, I suppose. What's the problem, exactly?'

'Well, Mark Zephyr's stuff is in wonderful order,' said Fran. 'It's in all those box files.

'Those stayed together.'

'Yes. And he was a careful worker. So in a way there isn't a problem . . . the other stuff *ought* to be the raw materials; Summerfield's papers from which Zephyr was working. But look at this.' Fran showed Imogen a thick, board-bound A4 notebook, nearly full of notes and script. 'Chapter One – Early childhood', it said on the first page. Then it listed sources – a nanny's recollections, interviews with family, letters home from holidays abroad . . . Imogen skipped down the long list. Three pages in the notebook began:

Gideon Summerfield was born in 1918, into a family of non-conformist artisans, living in a working-class suburb of London called Palmer's Green. His father was a cobbler, and his mother a dressmaker, and he was the youngest of three sons. The exotic name

belies these simple origins, but is explained by his family's member-
ship of a break-away missionary church serving the London poor
– the Church of Christ the Carpenter – who were given to Bible
readings and to using Old Testament names. Gideon's brothers
were Seth, born 1916, and Isaiah, born 1910 . . .

'Well, this is a start on the job,' said Imogen. 'What's the problem?'
'It isn't in Zephyr's hand,' said Fran. 'That's all.'
'Are you sure? Perhaps he had a different style for jotting and for
faircopy.'
'Compare,' said Fran, showing Imogen a note from Zephyr to
Recktype and Diss. There wasn't any question really of the hand-
writing being that of the writer of the notebook, Imogen saw that at
once. Zephyr's was small, neat and rounded; the notebook hand was
bold and angular.
'Anyway,' Fran continued, 'all Zephyr's work was done on a
computer – it's all printout in that spotty kind of print.'
'So the work in the notebook . . .'
'Is by someone else.'
'Well, is that so odd?' Imogen asked. 'Perhaps someone in his family
had begun to jot down a recollection . . .'
'What I was hoping was that you would remember what was in this,'
said Fran, holding out to Imogen the mended file marked 'Recovered
from premises of May Swann'.
'I'm afraid I just guessed,' said Imogen. 'I put stuff in that handwriting – like the big notebook – in this file, and all the other
stuff just in a bundle. Sorry.'
'Oh it's not your fault, Imogen,' said Fran. 'It's just very confusing.
There's such a lot of it; and . . . well, I'm puzzled. Mark Zephyr
was supposed to be about ready to write this *magnum opus*. And he
had reduced the subject to order, so it seems. Look, here's a list of
sources in his spotty printout. It is stepping through Chapter One,
and everything has a reference – like this.' She showed Imogen a page
of Zephyr's notes. 'Childhood holidays. *Vide* MS no. 23'.
'Well, surely a lot of this mountain of stuff is original material.
Somewhere there will be something numbered 23 . . .'
'Help me look,' said Fran. 'So far I can't find a single one of the
originals numbered in any way.'
A short shuffle through Summerfield's diaries, childhood letters and
school reports, all piled on the lefthand end of the settee confirmed it.

If the documents had been numbered, it was not by having numbers written on them.

'Well, let's speculate,' said Imogen. 'Suppose this file contained an assortment of original documents, coming from May Swann, who was some friend or relative of Summerfield's. The "Return to JS" file contained some other stuff – family papers. Without help we are never going to be able to reconstruct what was in which; but that may not matter for the moment. The notebook is perhaps a family member's record intended to help Mark Zephyr . . .'

'I'm going to have to ask someone at the publishers if they know more about it, I suppose,' said Fran.

'Well . . . Perhaps don't hurry,' said Imogen. 'Unless you want to work only with the Zephyr files. I'll show you something.'

Imogen went downstairs and returned with the note from Recktype and Diss that had finished up propped on her dresser the day the parcel came.

'You weren't supposed to see most of this stuff,' Imogen pointed out.

Fran became incandescent with rage. 'That's intolerable!' she cried. 'How can they give me a job like that and not trust me with the documents? What the hell are they playing at? I could never do a good scholarly piece of work without seeing the materials! Bloody hell, Imogen . . .'

'Has it occurred to you, Fran,' asked Imogen, 'that it must be your professor they don't trust? They don't know anything about you, do they? You are flying under his colours, so to speak.'

Fran sobered up at once. 'Well, I wouldn't trust him far, myself,' she said. 'Somehow. Don't know why I'm saying that. But I did think this was a fair offer. And I do need it so badly . . .'

'It probably is a fair offer, love,' said Imogen. 'Probably some clot in the publishers didn't understand that you would need the documents; they just thought you would merrily write up Zephyr's material, and so that was all you needed. But if you do need the rest, why not work on it quietly at once, and not draw attention to it until someone notices you've got it?'

'Imogen, you are a real pal. Thank you. That's good advice, and I'll take it.'

'Well, I can't see that I've been much help really . . .'

'Just talking to you helps. Clears the head.'

'You make me sound like an embrocation, child!' protested

Imogen. 'I'm off for my walk. The golden morning wastes. Feel like coming?'

'With all this to master? You're joking!' said Fran. 'Leave me in my salt mine and enjoy yourself!'

Imogen drove off in her little car to the car park at Wimpole Hall, and set out to march round the inner circuit – she hadn't time now for the longer, woodland walk. The shorter walk was pleasant enough, with the nearest thing to hill views that Cambridgeshire offered. She walked briskly, and in half an hour was ascending the gentle slope through chalky white ploughed land to the folly, set among trees on the slight summit. The folly, which had been constructed ready-ruined, to spare the expense of time, and made of brick within, for economy, and clunch and stone without, for authenticity, commanded a wide sweep of the gentle countryside, and improved the prospect from the windows of the house. Imogen walked through the gateway in the ivy-mantled tower, to the little phoney courtyard within, and saw at once a back she recognized – Lady B., sitting in contemplation on a low stretch of folly wall. Imogen crossed the grassy keep, and sat down beside her. A pair of little dogs came running up wagging and woofing in greeting, and Lady Buckmote looked round and smiled.

'Oh, Imogen! Are you the answer to a matron's prayer?'

'Depends what the matron happens to be praying for,' said Imogen, cautiously. 'If you want to share the driving on one of your hare-brained expeditions to the other end of England, definitely not.'

'No, no. Don't alarm yourself. I only want someone to make up the numbers at dinner. To be honest, I want a woman. I hate being the only female in these august gatherings. Tomorrow night; are you free?'

'I'm free, and female; but not specially august,' said Imogen. 'What's the occasion?'

'William wants to take a look at the new professor. The biography one with the funny name . . .'

'Maverack?'

'That's him. He has a chair, but no fellowship. The University is discreetly looking for a college to take him under its wing. William wants to dine with him before taking a view on that. He's invited various of our senior members . . .'

'I'd love to come,' said Imogen.

'You would?' Lady B. looked curiously at Imogen.

'I'd quite like a look at Dr Maverack. He's supervising Fran's PhD. I shall hear quite a lot about him these two years or more.'

'Fran?'

'Frances Bullion. My lodger.'

'Come for a quiet drink first then – sixish? We will stiffen our nerves for the evening.'

The two friends rose, and began the descent towards the model farm, and the return loop to the car park, with Lady B.'s long-haired dachshunds scampering ahead of them. At the gate to the last field Lady B. put the dogs on leads, as they walked between the strange-looking, curly-horned, long-horned, antique cattle in which the Wimpole farm specialised, under the lugubrious solemn gaze of these endangered creatures.

'That one,' said Lady B., pointing at a rough-haired, rather pale buff-coloured creature, with tight curls around its horns, 'reminds me of William.'

They looked at the amiable, baffled expression on the bullock's face and began to giggle together.

Imogen went home cheerful. She found Fran, sitting beside the Rayburn in the breakfast room, her slippered feet propped on the warm rail, her chair tipped up on its back feet, gently and thoughtfully rocking herself in the warmth of the stove.

'Sorted?' Imogen asked her.

'Not so's you'd notice. Not sorted as such,' said Fran, weightily. 'But I got clued up about one thing, at least.'

'Tell,' said Imogen, hanging her coat in the cupboard, and sitting down in the facing chair.

'I found this.' Fran held out to Imogen several pages of yellow ruled paper stapled together at the top. It was a neatly written and carefully numbered list. Against the numbers were brief descriptions – postcard, dated 23.4.68, picture Brighton Pier ... Letter from Simon Brown, dated 3.9.68 ... Imogen looked down the page for number 23. 'Postcard from G.S. to Aunt Emily; Postmark New Romney 5.6.79.'

'So those manuscript numbers in Mark Zephyr's list . . .'

'Were numbers assigned in this list. Yes; I've checked. They correspond.'

'So you should be able to sort out the stuff with the help of this list?' Genuinely though Imogen was interested in Fran, she wasn't a historian, or an archivist, and her mind was wandering towards the consideration of what was in the house for supper.

'Well, yes. Though I still wouldn't know which lot of things were labelled "Return to JS".'

'Does that matter?'

'Well yes, it might.'

'I do see that if JS turned up demanding the return of documents, and you didn't know which were hers . . .'

'Why do you say "hers"?'

'Well, I was jumping to conclusions, I suppose. But isn't Mrs Gideon Summerfield a J? I thought she was called Janet.'

'Aha!' said Fran. 'I hadn't tumbled to that yet. So very likely then, she is the JS to whom stuff must be returned. Or rather, some of the stuff. Makes sense.'

'But you were explaining to me why it might matter ahead of the embarrassment if the documents get reclaimed.'

'Well, take number 48 on the list, for example,' said Fran. 'It's a postcard from Chartres. It isn't signed. It isn't addressed. It just says, "Enclosing this to remind you – it's as wonderful as you said it was. See you next term, Yours ever, M." So there's nothing to connect it with Summerfield at all. But it is evidence that he went to Chartres.'

'Lots of people have been to Chartres . . .'

'Oh, it isn't that it's in any way unlikely, Imogen. But to use it you would have to know the provenance of the postcard. If you saw it quoted in a biography a footnote would say, "From a card enclosed in a letter from Peter X, circa 1978," or something. If the card was given to the biographer by the great man's wife, having been found among his papers, one would be satisfied that it really had been written to him; if you don't know from Adam where the card came from, then it doesn't prove anything. It might have got accidentally picked up among other papers from a colleague's desk; it might have been sent to Mark Zephyr and just got muddled with his Summerfield stuff; it might have been planted . . .'

'Fran, why in heaven or earth would anyone plant a postcard that falsely proved that Summerfield had been to Chartres?'

'Well, they wouldn't, of course. That was just an example, a hypothetical instance to demonstrate to you that you have to know where documents came from; who has owned them between the time they date from and their coming into your hands, before you can rely on them. It's a fundamental principle of historical research. You'd be surprised how often in the history of history people have planted evidence, or suppressed it, or cunningly omitted it.'

'And is biography history? We could have macaroni cheese, if you're eating with me tonight. I can put tinned tunny fish in it.'

'Brill,' said Fran. 'I'll set the table. But Imogen, what I'm trying to tell you is, this list is in the second hand.'

'Second hand? As on a clock face, or as in a junk shop? I don't get you.'

'Neither. As in a taxonomy of handwriting. Fran Bullion's own classification. To wit: first hand Mark Zephyr's writing. Small, rounded, neat. Betrays tidy mind. Very little of it; most of his stuff is in spotty printout.'

'Like the list of MS materials you showed me earlier?'

'Exactly. That list uses numbers which are in this list – here on the yellow paper – and this list is in the second hand, bold, angular, strong-looking, uses blue-black real ink.'

'And whose is the second hand?' asked Imogen, putting a pan of water on to boil, cooking while she listened.

'Well, I rather think,' said Fran, getting up from the chair, and coming to lean against the side of the door into the little kitchen, 'that I can say with some certainty. Those Zephyr references to "MS" number 23, don't mean "manuscript number 23", you see. Later in his list we get references to manuscript material called "IG number suchwhich". MS means May Swann. And if this list was written by May Swann, then it all fits perfectly. All Zephyr's references to "MS" numbers correspond to the numbers in this list. And, Imogen, if this list is in May Swann's handwriting, then so is the work in the big notebook – the Chapter One, you remember – and various other things, including pages of notes. Which make it perfectly clear to me that May Swann, whoever she was, had a lot of the great Gideon Summerfield's private papers in her hands, and had carefully listed them, and begun putting biographical facts in a notebook, and where is she now?'

'She must have given up on the job and handed the papers back,' said Imogen. 'Cut some brown bread for me, will you, Fran?'

4

Sir William Buckmote, the Master of St Agatha's College, greeted Imogen warmly. 'Sit down, sit down Imogen. Sherry? How kind of you to share the ordeal of the evening with us.'

'Will it be an ordeal?' asked Imogen, smiling at him, and accepting the proffered glass. 'Satisfying one's curiosity is usually a pleasure, even if one is also appalled . . .'

'But what is it about the reputedly dreadful Professor Maverack that has so aroused the curiosity of both you and my dear wife?' the Master enquired, sitting down comfortably with his own sherry. 'I have come to associate a common front between you two with trouble for the college; it fills me with dread.'

'William! How grossly unfair of you,' said Lady B. 'Take it back at once!'

'Shan't,' said the Master, smiling gleefully at his wife. 'You two were in cahoots during the whole of that unfortunate affair over the Wyndham Case.'

'Just as well we were,' said Lady B. crisply. 'We saved the college face in more ways than one.'

'Of course my dear, of course. You are wholly benign, and so is our dear Imogen; it's just the feeling you give me of something *going on*; you know how I hate goings on. I am happiest when the nearest happening of any kind is several million light years away, and the college is safely sunk in the somnolence of centuries.'

'Oh, go along with you, William,' said Lady B., in sweetly feigned crossness.

'Something is going on, just the same,' the Master observed. 'Humour me; put my mind at rest. Tell me why the Master's wife and the college nurse are on parade to inspect Professor Maverack. Who is, as I say, reputedly dreadful.'

'We didn't know his reputation,' said Imogen. 'In what way is he supposed to be dreadful?'

'Well, if he were personable and charming he wouldn't be handed round from college to college looking for somewhere to give him a fellowship,' said the Master.

'Oh, but William you know perfectly well the trouble isn't about Professor Maverack *personally*; it's just that people wonder about biography as the subject for a professorship . . .'

'Well, I'm just a humble astrophysicist,' said the Master, grinning wickedly. 'You can't expect me to understand what's wrong with biography as a subject. Naturally I assumed that the subject was impeccable, and that the trouble must be caused by the man . . .'

'Arguments *ad hominem* are famously dicey,' said Imogen. 'Surely that's true in astrophysics?'

'Oh, quite, my dear Imogen, quite. But in biography, whatever else could arguments be?'

'*Ad feminam*, perhaps?' she said.

'Oh, no!' he said. '*Homo, hominem* distinguished a man from beasts and angels. *Vir, virum* distinguished a man from a woman. But you see what I mean.'

'Don't admit a thing,' said Lady B. 'And William, dear, isn't it time to go in and face the subject?'

'Lord, so it is,' said the Master, swiftly finishing his sherry, and rising. He took his gown from the back of his chair, and struggled into it, arms waving like the wings of a raven, and then led the way through his private door into the Combination Room, where the company for dinner assembled.

Dr Maverack was a round-faced man in middle age, with receding red hair, and gold-framed spectacles. He had bushy eyebrows, and a darting glance from pale blue eyes. His evening shirt was rather elaborate, with starched ruffles, and he was wearing gold cuff-links in the form of tiny curled dragons with pinhead rubies for eyes. He was surrounded by St Agatha's dons when the Master's party entered; hanging back a little Imogen remained on the edge of the group, watching. Those lavish cuff-links caught her eye while she studied him. The Master hastened forward, extending a hand in greeting, and asking if everyone had been introduced.

'Ah, here is Lanyard now,' he said, as a late-comer arrived. 'Lanyard is our Director of Studies in English Literature, Dr Maverack . . .'

The gathered company exchanged small-talk.

'How are you finding Cambridge, Dr Maverack?' asked the Master.

'A little daunting, if the truth be told,' said Dr Maverack.

'You have come to us from . . .?'

'San Diego. And before that, Williams.'

'Williams?' enquired Lanyard.

'Western Massachusetts,' said Maverack.

'Well, no doubt you would find our entrenched traditionalism daunting . . .' said Lanyard.

'I like the traditions,' said Maverack. 'It's the traffic that terrifies me!'

Everyone laughed. 'The thing to do,' said the Dean, 'is to find a college conveniently in the centre of things, and preferably not on the Backs, unless one is able to love one's fellow men in very large numbers and assorted nationalities, and simply not own a car. Walk everywhere; it's much better for your health.'

'Excellent advice,' said Maverack. 'I hope to follow it. But of course, I am being selected rather than selecting when it comes to a college address.'

'I hope your welcome in the department has been friendly?' asked Plomer, St Agatha's second English fellow. Did Maverack know Plomer had been stubbornly opposed to a chair in Biography? Imogen wondered. If so he showed no sign of it.

'Friendly, but cautious,' he said, smiling.

'And you have some research students?' the Master asked. 'You have, so to speak, a clientèle for the subject?'

'Oh, yes,' said Maverack. 'Young brains take to it easily; it's the older minds who think that a footnote or two in the history of literature will cover the matter well enough.'

Just as the butler announced that dinner was served, Imogen noticed that there was a third woman in the room – an elegantly dressed middle-aged woman with smoothly upswept hair, standing quietly in a far corner, apparently engrossed in contemplation of the college's portrait of Christopher Wyndham. Imogen stepped over to her as the company massed at the doors, and began the informal procession to the table.

'Who was Christopher Wyndham?' the woman asked. 'Ought I to know? Well, I don't know anybody here, so perhaps it's not surprising . . .'

'I am Imogen Quy,' said Imogen. 'I am the college nurse.'

'Holly Portland,' said the other, holding out a hand.

'Are you someone's guest?' asked Imogen.

'Not exactly. I am working in Cambridge for a few weeks, and

St Agatha's offered me dining rights. I thought I'd try it . . .'

'Come with me, and I'll show you how it works,' said Imogen, leading Holly to the rear of the rapidly diminishing press of people at the Combination Room door. 'It isn't usually as crowded as this. Everyone has turned out to see if they want Dr Maverack as a fellow.'

Holly Portland smiled. 'Never mind Leo Maverack,' she said. 'I was at grad school with him. I can't take him entirely seriously; tell me about Christopher Wyndham.' She had a soft, but clearly sounding American accent.

'A college benefactor, contemporary with Isaac Newton,' said Imogen.

'An ultra conservative, I take it,' said Holly Portland, smiling again.

'Well, yes; but how do you know?' asked Imogen, leading the way onto the dais at the head of the hall. Two long trestles stood ready laid out with rows of silver candlesticks, shining flatware and crystal glasses. The floor of the hall was bright with warm lights at all the tables, and the undergraduates were already seated; above everyone's heads the magnificent beamed roof rose into shadows, darkening towards the ridge, far above the gilt-framed portraits, and the linenfold panelling.

Holly's eyes widened. As the diners filed in and stood behind the chairs at the tables she found herself opposite Imogen, with Lanyard beside her. 'Your Christopher Wyndham is shown with a Ptolemaic astrolabe,' she said. 'That makes him conservative at least; more likely very reactionary.'

The Dean read grace, and everyone sat down.

'Has it occurred to you that the man might have been painted with his astrolabe *before* the publication of Newton's *Principia?*' asked Lanyard.

'I think the portrait was painted in 1692, give or take a year,' said Holly firmly.

'We'll ask the experts,' said Lanyard, calling diagonally across the table to Dr Bagadeuce. 'Meredith, when was our Wyndham portrait painted?'

'1691, I think,' Dr Bagadeuce replied. 'Miss Quy, have you met Li Tao?' He indicated a young man of oriental appearance, sitting opposite. 'Li Tao is joining us for a year, doing research into mathematics.'

'I hope you'll be very happy with us,' said Imogen. 'What is your research project?'

'Ah, the ABC conjecture,' Li Tao said.

'Is that important?' asked Imogen. She could think only of the ABC murders.

'Oh, yes,' said Li Tao, 'it is very strong. It implies Fermat's last theorem.'

'But what is that?' asked Holly.

'Ah, is great mystery,' said Li Tao. 'Fermat left note, saying he had found proof. Nobody knows what proof was.'

But now the soup was served, and as serious conversation began at the top of the table, a hush spread down towards where Imogen was sitting. People were listening in, as far as the medieval acoustics allowed them to, but the truth was that the length of the table kept conversations rather local; the Master's conversation was out of earshot.

'Can't hear what the fellow is saying,' muttered Lanyard, crossly. 'We'll have to buttonhole him over port, I think.'

'Tell me what you are working on in Cambridge,' said Imogen to Holly Portland.

'Eighteenth-century Indian calicos,' Holly said. 'There's your conversation stopper. You'd better tell me about being a college nurse.'

'Alas,' said Imogen, smiling, 'all the interesting bits are highly confidential. But why should your subject stop conversation? *I'm* interested. I wouldn't have thought there'd be many eighteenth-century calicos left.'

'No, there aren't. Sometimes the only knowledge we have of a fabric is from a tiny scrap left in a seam. My work is in establishing criteria for dating fabric; even the smallest scraps might be useful.'

As the meal progressed from soup to fish to racks of lamb, to elaborate choux pastry birds filled with fruit and cream, Imogen kept Holly talking. They were soon talking about quilts. Evidence for dating fabrics often came from dated quilts; once known it would often help to date undated quilts. From 1700, when tariffs were imposed in England to help protect English silks, linen and wool from hugely popular Indian cottons, with their bright permanent colours, there were also descriptions – records of goods seized from smugglers by the excise men, for example. One could get some idea from such records of what designs and colours were popular. The exorbitantly expensive indigo dyes, for example, were often mentioned.

Imogen, of course, was more interested in contemporary quilts, although she knew what a long tradition they were in. Holly was less interested in fabrics, or in quilts in the twentieth century; dating them got much easier, with the manufacturers' catalogues, and fashion magazines, and so forth often allowing exact knowledge of a particular print. The whirlwind of changes in fashionable taste meant that modern fabrics were marketed for quite short times – perhaps only for a single season, and then went out of production.

'It might be many years, though,' said Imogen, thoughtfully, 'before something made into a shirt, say, and then worn, and then finally tossed into the scrap bag, was pulled out and made part of a quilt. Mightn't it be forty or fifty years?'

'Well, the date the fabric was first sold gives the earliest possible date for a quilt – or a shirt for that matter. The latest possible date would be harder; but it isn't very likely someone would make a quilt entirely out of very old shirts. You could usually get the earliest possible date from one fabric and the latest possible from another. Dyes fade, and fabric wears; an expert can date things pretty well.'

The absolute eldorado for Holly, Imogen gathered, was to find in an American quilt a fabric or design which undoubtedly came from England, so settling the controversy over whether the tradition crossed the Atlantic with early settlers, or developed independently in the New World. She wasn't very likely to succeed; the earliest known patchwork was in bed-hangings at Levens Hall in Cumberland, dating from 1708.

When the meal was over and a closing grace was said, the company left the great hall, and crossed the Fountain Court to the Combination Room, where dessert and port and coffee awaited them. In this less formal setting people moved around freely, changed places, joined or left conversations as they pleased.

Rather as Imogen had expected, when she and Holly entered the room the Master was leading Dr Maverack to a central chair at the great oval table, where everyone could see and hear him. The senior members were assiduously plying their guests with choices of port or claret, fruit or nuts, and offering histories of the silver laid out before them – that splendid candlestand, Dr Bagadeuce was saying, was the only piece of college silver to pre-date the Civil War. Cromwell's men had reoccupied the castle, which formed part of the college buildings, and comprehensively sacked it. They had found all the college treasure and stolen it, melting it down for army pay. The candlestick alone had escaped, hidden in a cartload of books that the Master and scholars had been permitted to take with them to Barnwell, where they sat out the Civil War. The candlestick was duly admired. It was a ring of dancing angels, a gothicised vision of a Renaissance three graces, with wings. The angels circled, each with one hand upraised holding a candle, and the other holding an undulant banner bearing the inscription '*Lumen ad revelationem gentium*'. All the courtesies accomplished, the business of the evening was launched by the Master.

'Are you engaged in writing a biography at present, Dr Maverack?'

'Not at present, no.'

'But you have someone in your sights, I presume? May we enquire whom?'

'At present, nobody. It is some little time since I wrote a biography. I have written only three altogether.'

'Let me see,' said Lanyard. 'A life of a Duke of Northumberland; a life of Carmichael, the Victorian landscape painter, and a life of Sir Humphrey Davy. Am I right?'

'You are perfectly right,' said Dr Maverack, 'but I imagine you have been reading *Who's Who* rather than the books in question.'

Lanyard smiled. 'A useful work,' he said.

'Oh, very. But you see, Lanyard, even a man as well read and distinguished as yourself is likely to read a biography only if for some reason he is very interested in the subject of it. One may labour for years to write a scholarly biography of some nineteenth-century figure, even a fairly important one, and win very few readers.'

'You surprise me, Dr Maverack,' said Lady B. 'Every time I go into Heffers, it seems to me, I find tables groaning under the weight of new biographies. Surely the publishers' catalogues are full of them?'

'Popular biography, like popular fiction, does do quite well,' Dr Maverack told her. 'One should not deplore it, I think. Fine scholarship is bound to be a minority taste.'

'Oh, I wasn't deploring it,' said Lady B., quietly.

'You do not seem hugely enthusiastic about biography, for a man who has just been appointed to the only chair in it,' remarked Mr Sykes, St Agatha's Senior History Don.

'Ah, well, I am a theoretician myself, rather than a practitioner,' said Dr Maverack.

'There is a *theory* of biography?' said Lanyard. 'I would have thought that of all subjects it would be the most circumstantial and particular. Of what possible use can a theory be?'

'Why, my dear fellow, one can't write a word without one!' said Dr Maverack, suddenly animated. 'How can one propound the meaning of a human life without a theory of what makes human life meaning-ful? Everything you decide to include, or to exclude, the very choice of whose life is worth attention implies a philosophy – indeed embodies a philosophy. One might indeed suggest – I think I would suggest – that the history of the theory of biography is the history of western moral philosophy. It is, I assure you, very much more interesting than any particular human life, even the greatest.'

He had certainly got the attention of everyone present now.

'Can you give us an example of the interaction of theory and biography?' asked the Master.

'Easily,' Dr Maverack replied. 'We might start at the beginning with Plutarch. He was interested only in world leaders – and what inter-ested him about them was their style of leadership. His comparisons between great Greeks and great Romans was intended to provide a copybook of examples in how and how not to rule. It certainly didn't occur to him that the private lives of his subjects was of any interest except in so far as it might account for some public action. And one would imagine he would have dismissed as of no possible interest the life of anyone who held no public office of any kind.'

'You mean that he had a theory of human value which esteemed only powerful men?' asked Mr Sykes.

'Precisely. But when we move into the Dark Ages we get a com-pletely different set of values. What is important in a deeply Christian society is redemption – an account of an inner life, full of conversion stories, full of bright lights on roads to Damascus. The biographies become plentiful, and many of them are of very humble folk. They are so strange to us we have coined a special name for them – hagiography. And the lives of the saints laid down such a powerful pattern that the few lives of laymen which survive – like Asser's Life of Alfred, or the Life of Charlemagne – make peculiar attempts to force the life stories of vigorous military kings into the saint's life shape. If we are to believe Asser, Alfred was a sickly and pious boy. But most likely this is because the only model for a meaningful life story which Asser had, was hagiography. Alfred was clearly as tough as old rope.'

'Well, bring us to a more modern stage,' said Lanyard. 'How does this story go on?'

'Boswell, obviously, is the first modern biographer,' said Dr Maverack. 'By his time the idea of character has emerged; the idea of human beings as specimens, individuals. An individual is valued

32

for colour, eccentricity; the biographer works by valiant attempts at total inclusion. An inclusion, however, untroubled by the privacy of sexual life; presumably a man's sexuality was not seen as specially important – and therefore as not specially informative about him.'

'Until Freud puts sexuality in the centre of things?' said Max Allotson, the Fellow in Psychology.

'Exactly!' cried Dr Maverack joyfully. 'Of course not everybody in our times is a Freudian, and so you do get people calling biographers muck-rakers or worse when they go pounding after the sexual history of their subjects, and relatives, heirs and assigns get very upset, and literary executors turn themselves into angry censors; but what is going on is strictly theoretical; a theory of life which puts sexuality at the heart of human personality.'

'Freudian interpretation must by now be on the wane, surely?' asked Lanyard. 'What will take its place, do you think, Dr Maverack?'

'Deconstruction,' said Dr Maverack briskly. 'A theory that human life has no meaning at all.'

'Well, but in that case why would anyone write biography?' asked Lanyard.

'I suppose there is a historical value in the discovery and ordering of archives and materials,' said Sykes.

'One of our greatest biographers, Leon Edel,' said Dr Maverack, 'called that sort of thing the kitchen work of the task. According to him the true task is to discover the lies and delusions by which all men and women defend themselves against the indignities of life, and expose them. To deconstruct, if you like, the pitiful walls of the castle of self-respect people build for themselves. I agree with him.'

'You seem to be implying,' said the Dean, 'that there are no truths by which anyone could live; no simple people finding meaning in their lives but not deceiving themselves.'

'Yes,' said Dr Maverack, smiling. 'Byron said he thought that people lied to themselves more than to other people. He was right.'

'But do you mean that all systems of meaning that attribute value to human life are false?' A note of outrage had entered the Dean's voice.

'Well, there are so many they cannot all be true, and possibly none are,' said Dr Maverack. 'In any case, the fundamental point is simply that people lie to themselves, to keep the thought of chaos, or of their own futility, at bay. No doubt some lies are more profitable than others, some disguises less crippling than others.'

'But there is no such thing as human merit or real achievement, or solidly based self-respect?' asked the Master. He sounded more amused than outraged. Had Dr Maverack missed the fact that in advancing his theory to the assembled senior members of St Agatha's College, Cambridge, loaded with academic and political honours as they were, he was putting it to people who had a lot to lose if he was right? 'Not a very uplifting thought, if I may say so,' the Master added.

'But did you expect a Professor of Biography to cheer you up?' asked Dr Maverack. 'Or to bolster your self-esteem? Surely not.'

'I told you not to take any notice of Leo Maverack,' murmured Holly to Imogen. 'He's a leading exemplar of his own theory.'

But Imogen, who had for some reason been expecting to take against Dr Maverack, was rather impressed by him. She had noticed him several times during the evening glancing appreciatively at her. He had a pleasantly eager demeanour. And there was no denying he was a lively talker.

5

Zephyr, Imogen reflected the next morning, cannot be a common name. But she had been at school with a Pamela Zephyr, many years ago. She could clearly remember an anxious little girl with blue hair slides in black hair, who struggled to rise above her alphabetical order in the weekly achievement scores read out in assembly. Imogen hadn't thought of her or seen her for years; even the appearance of the surname on the Summerfield file hadn't immediately triggered memory. Idly, now, she looked her up in the phone book. And there, among the Zacs, and Zawadas and Zinofiefs was a Zephyr. In Waterbeach – not far at all. Imogen tried to think of some sort of pretext to break the ice. But when none occurred to her she boldly dialled the number anyway.

And it was unexpectedly easy. A woman's voice answered.

'Am I speaking to Pamela Zephyr?' Imogen asked.

'Yes. And I am not buying encyclopaedias or double glazing,' said the voice.

'This is Imogen Quy, Pamela.'

'Good gracious – I remember you – you did my maths for me at school.'

'Did I? I hope I got it right.'

'Better than I could, anyway. How are you these days? Where are you?'

'I'm flourishing in Cambridge. Pamela, is Mark Zephyr a relative of yours?'

There was a pause. Then an answer in an altered tone of voice. 'Yes. He's – he was – my brother.'

Imogen was startled. She had expected, she couldn't think quite why, a father or an uncle. 'Can I come and talk to you about him? Some time fairly soon?'

'You can come and talk about anything. Come now if you like. I'm very lonely.'

'I'm due in college in half an hour. If I drove out to you after work I'd arrive around three. How would that be?'

'Lovely. I'll expect you.'

Imogen had a quiet day in college. The high point was a swift exchange of views with Lady B. 'Was he so terrible, did you think?' Lady B. had asked, putting her head round Imogen's office door.

'That rather depends on the field of comparison,' said Imogen cautiously.

'Well – as dons go?'

'I'd say I'd known worse,' said Imogen.

'At St Agatha's?'

'I don't think he'd strike an all-time low here, do you?'

'Hmm. No, not really. But I don't think they're minded to have him, just the same.'

'Well, he does seem like a strong sort of flavour,' Imogen said.

'Did you notice that he didn't mention Summerfield, when they asked what he was working on?'

'Yes, I did. Odd that, when Summerfield was . . .'

'A St Agatha's man. Yes, that's what I thought. Perhaps because your student friend is doing all the work?'

'Well, but Maverack's name is to go on the book, as I understand.'

'Well then, perhaps,' said Lady B., 'it's natural embarrassment about that which stopped him mentioning it. Must fly. Come for a coffee tomorrow? Just before your office hours?'

'Tenish, then,' said Imogen. 'Love to.'

Driving out to Pamela Zephyr's house, with a bunch of chrysanths in the car, Imogen reflected. She had unconsciously been assuming that Mark Zephyr, if dead, had been elderly. Wrong, it seemed, unless Pamela's family had had remarkably spread out children, or Mark had been a step-brother. She resolved to be very tactful with Pamela.

At first, when Pamela opened the door of the house – a pleasant Victorian villa, set back from the road – Imogen thought she would not have recognised her. Her dark hair was greying at the temples, and drawn back into a bun. She still wore hair slides – an elegant pair of tortoiseshell ones, smoothing her hair above the ears. She was smiling. 'Come in, do come in,' she said. 'Oh it's such a treat to see you after all these years!'

She took Imogen's coat, and led her into a pretty, cluttered sitting-room, where afternoon tea was set out on a side-table – a lavish tea with Florentines, and cucumber sandwiches, and an elaborate cake. 'Oh, you shouldn't have taken so much trouble . . .' said Imogen. 'It isn't every day one rediscovers an old friend,' said Pamela, still smiling. 'Or, indeed, sees a friend at all,' she added sadly. Suddenly Imogen recognised her – saw the expression of anxiety that she remembered so well on the little girl's face settle down on the face of the grown woman. When Pamela said, 'You haven't changed much, Imogen,' she answered, 'Neither have you,' and they both laughed merrily.

'How did we lose touch?' asked Imogen, accepting sandwiches, and a cup of tea.

'When you went to America. You did give me an address, but I lost it when we moved house.'

'That must be it. I didn't stay in America long. My engagement came unstuck. I'm still in the house in Newnham.'

'Mark and I moved here soon after you left,' said Pamela. 'You wanted to ask about Mark, but you didn't say why.'

'Someone I'm very fond of has taken over the Summerfield biography,' said Imogen.

'Well, stop them if you can. It was a horrible job. It was practically the death of Mark.'

'It was the death of Mark?' asked Imogen. She couldn't help the appalled note in her voice.

'Oh, not literally of course. Just that it clouded his last days, and I do so bitterly resent that now. *Then* of course, we didn't know it was his last days.'

Imogen said, 'You mustn't let me upset you, Pamela. I'm sorry to come raising painful queries. But I would be very grateful if you would tell me about it all.'

'People don't understand, you know,' said Pamela, getting up and wandering off to stand gazing into her garden through the french windows. 'People are surprised one should be so devastated by the death of a brother. Once one is a grown-up. I rather wonder whether I really am a grown-up. But Mark always looked after me. In lots of ways. He paid the bills, and organised things, and arranged our holidays, and brought his friends over to meet me. He looked after me ever since school, when he used to fight the boys who teased me. That's why he moved in here with me when his wife left him. She kept the house, and the children. Mark moved in here. And we were very happy, Imogen, really we were, in spite of people telling us

37

it wouldn't work. There must be a lot of crummy families around, I think, for people to be surprised when brother and sister get on.'

'I'm not surprised,' said Imogen. 'Just jealous. I'm an only child. And I'm afraid I don't remember Mark. Was he much older than you?'

'No; he was two years younger. That's why it was so plucky of him to fight for me; he had to take on boys much older than himself.'

'Did he win these fights?'

'Usually, yes. He was quite tiny, but he got so furiously angry! They called him little spitfire, and kept clear of him!' She was smiling again at the recollection.

'Pamela, what was so awful about the Summerfield job?'

'In a word, or two words rather, Janet Summerfield,' said Pamela.

'Summerfield's widow?'

'That vitriolic, vicious, unhinged harpy!' said Pamela. 'She's deranged. She didn't want a biography, she wanted a hagiography. And Mark wasn't her man; not for that kind of job. She would come storming out here shouting about writs and copyright, and trying to take back documents, and demanding the right to check every word he wrote . . . He actually ran away from her, Imogen, would you believe that? That a man could be driven into hiding from his own house? God, it was awful.'

'Why didn't he just chuck it in? If, in effect, she was making it impossible?'

'Little spitfire, remember? He hated defeat. And unfairness, and unreasonable conduct. And another thing, I'm afraid. He needed the money rather badly. He was paying alimony, and his eldest daughter was at a private school . . .'

'Don't apologise. Why shouldn't he do a job for money?' said Imogen. 'It's a clean, clear, honourable motive. There are a lot of messier reasons for writing a biography, I think.'

'It's good to talk to you,' said Pamela. 'You have a nice clear mind, without being a cold person. Do you know what that hell-cat did in the end? You can't imagine, Imogen! She sent a solicitor with a court order and two heavies round here *the day after Mark died* to recover the Summerfield papers. The very next day! I was terrified. And of course, I hadn't a clue which of Mark's papers were his, and which had anything to do with Summerfield. They were just clearing his desk – sweeping things into cardboard crates – it was terrible. Luckily my neighbour is a lawyer – a judge, as it happens, and I ran out of the back door and fetched him. By the time he came the cardboard crates were lined up in the hall ready to go off in their car, but Max stopped them, and made them put most of it back. They were way outside their rights.'

'I should think so!' said Imogen, appalled.

'They said they were going to sort out everything back at their office and return anything not to do with Summerfield later. But Max made them sort right there, so that they couldn't take anything not to do with Summerfield. There was a lot of argument. They had actually impounded Mark's cheque book. Max talked a lot, and when his son came to see what was taking so long, he sent him to fetch the cricket team, who were all in the pavilion, and they all came over and stood around, holding their bats. That speeded things up a bit. The hell-cat's lawyer said it was threatening behaviour, and Max said how did he think he would demonstrate in court that it was threatening behaviour for a village cricket team to hold bats just before a game, right beside a cricket field?' Pamela smiled ruefully.

'Do you have any idea what was worrying her about Mark's work?' asked Imogen.

'Not really. I don't think he had uncovered any scandals – he kept complaining how boring the man was. And he was a good way through the work, too. There were just one or two loose ends to tie up, he said, and then he could complete the thing in draft, and get on with polishing up a finished version.'

'And then . . .? What happened?'

'He went to see her. He was hoping to calm her down, and get things sorted out. There was just one thing he needed to know from her, he said. He thought she must know it . . .'

'You don't know what that was?'

'Something to do with holidays. I didn't follow it all. And it must have worked – his charm offensive, I mean, because he came back very cheerful and happy, quite like his old self, and swept me off to dinner at a posh restaurant, and we had a lovely time. Then when we got back to the car he was suddenly feeling tired, so I drove us home, and he went straight to bed. Then he couldn't sleep. He was feverish and he woke me staggering around fetching himself water. I called the doctor out first thing in the morning, and he shot Mark into hospital. But he was unconscious before he got there, and he died some time in the afternoon. I try to tell myself that there's a lot to be said for a rapid death, but it was a terrible shock to me, as you can imagine.'

'What was it? Meningitis? Food poisoning?'

'I honestly don't know. They thought it was meningitis, but their scanner was busy, and he was dead before they could get him on to it. I thought only children died of meningitis, but I must be wrong.'

'There have been some minor epidemics recently, I think. Pamela, I'm so sorry. You really have had a bad time.'

'I'm getting over it. Slowly. One of the problems is having nobody to do things with. Mark liked walking, and we went somewhere every weekend; somehow there doesn't seem enough point on one's own.'

'Well, I like walking too,' said Imogen. 'Let's go into partnership over that. Do you know the circuit of Linton Hill and the Roman road?'

'Yes; but I haven't been there for some time.'

'What about next Saturday, then? And a pub lunch?'

'Oh, that would be a treat! Are you sure you have time?'

'I've only just rediscovered you,' said Imogen. 'We have a lot of time to make up.'

Later as Imogen was leaving, Pamela said, 'Watch out for that friend of yours, won't you?'

'Yes, I will. But you said Mark had nearly done it all. So Fran hasn't a huge task ahead?'

'A few loose ends. And dealing with an unhinged widow. I don't know; perhaps it was just Mark that got on her wick, and she will be all sweet reason with another person. Perhaps. Mark often wondered how his predecessor had got on with the dreadful Janet, but of course we couldn't ask her.'

Imogen was standing in the hall, putting on her coat when Pamela said this; she froze to the spot. 'His predecessor?' she asked.

'Oh, didn't you know? Mark wasn't the first person to work on the Summerfield book. A lot of the work was already done when he took it on.'

'Who was it, before Mark?'

'One May Swann.'

'And what . . .?'

'She disappeared. I kept hoping she'd turn up again, and take the project back; we could have managed without the money *somehow*. But she didn't.'

'Pamela, people don't just disappear . . .'

'Well, I wouldn't have thought so either. But it seems they do. The police have great long lists. She just went out one morning, I understand, and didn't come back. Hasn't been heard of since. Odd, that.'

Or worse, thought Imogen, driving herself home, concentrating intently on the road. They can't do a breath test to discover that you were out of your mind with worry, or in shock when you were driving, but either can be as dangerous as drink. She did her level best to drive safely, and got hooted at for what seemed to the driver in the car behind her excessive caution at the A45 crossover. And all the while her mind was intoning to her, 'Odd, or worse.'

6

The problem was whether to say anything to Fran. And if so what, exactly. And what moment to choose. When Imogen got in from visiting Pamela, Fran could be heard all over the house, singing in the bath. What a horrible job it would be to persuade her that her wonderful job was booby-trapped! Imogen thought perhaps she would react strongly against advice – who could blame her? Would Imogen herself have taken cautious, middle-aged advice in such a situation? And what exactly needed saying to Fran? She already knew that an earlier worker had died in harness.

Imogen sat down after supper, and took her notebook from the bookcase. She drew a line under the previous entries, which were all about the death of an undergraduate last year. A sticky label on the front of the book said 'Patient Histories'. When troubled in her mind, or when something needed carefully thinking through, Imogen often retreated to the discipline she had learned as a student nurse. You wrote down everything the patient had told you, and everything you had observed, and tried to make sense of it. Now she headed a page 'The Life of Summerfield', and began to write, not, oddly, in her current, bold, rapid calligraphy with a thick-nibbed pen – the way she wrote letters to friends – but in the careful neat, rounded and legible hand she had used as a nurse. It was always important that the next nurse on duty could read your notes – fast, if necessary.

So what did it all amount to? Summerfield was a near nonentity, except for one splendid piece of work . . . his biographers were unlucky. Mark Z. had died suddenly; his predecessor had vanished. Coincidence? Perhaps. And perhaps it was also a coincidence that his current biographer (official) had farmed out the job, taken cover, so to speak, behind a student. Imogen laid down her pencil and gazed at the flickering pastiche coal fire that burned serenely and undemandingly in the grate. There was a feel of farrago about what she had written. A feel of an imagination run riot. Imogen accused herself sternly. Was she bored? Had she acquired a ghoulish lust for excitement, so that now she was deliberately fomenting fear and suspicion? After some hesitation she gave herself a clean bill of health – she could reasonably tell herself that she was perfectly contented with the even tenor of her days – but she had nevertheless made a decision. It was too early to tell Fran anything. She must check further first.

By and by Fran appeared, rosy from her warm bath, and wrapped in a fluffy dressing-gown, offering to make hot chocolate. Imogen accepted, and the two of them listened to some Mozart together, and exchanged college gossip before bed.

When her college hours were over the next day, Imogen phoned a friend, Mike Parsons, Detective Sergeant in the Cambridgeshire police. Mike had taken a St John's Ambulance Brigade first aid course with Imogen, who had felt at the time she needed a refresher course in dealing with accidents. He had confided in her – his relationship with his wife had been shaky at the time – and they had become good friends with a habit of leaning on each other's expertise.

'I need a little help, Mike. How about a pub supper some time?'

'Is it urgent, old friend? Only I'm off to Lanzarote for a well-deserved week tomorrow. Before the season of mists gets going. Can it wait?'

'Of course,' she said, trying to disguise dismay.

'I perceive that the true answer is not really,' he said. 'Look, I absolutely must stay here and pack; but why don't you skither round here right away? I'll put the kettle on, and if you happened to pass Sainsbury's on the way you could bring some sandwiches.'

'Lunch service on its way,' said Imogen, ringing off.

Mike lived in a flat in Chesterton, not too far for Imogen's ancient bike, even with its basket full of juice and sandwiches. He greeted her at the door with, 'Can you iron, by any chance?' He had scalded a large, iron-shaped burn on the front of a polyester shirt.

'Indeed I can,' said Imogen marching in. Almost every flat surface in the living-room had clothes draped on it. A suitcase was open on the table, with a mountain of clothes piled up in it, and a pair of shoes and a pair of pyjamas topping it off.

'Where's Barbara?' asked Imogen at once. Mike had had a little trouble with his wife during the years she had known him.

'It's nothing like that,' he said. 'She's there already with her mother and the children. I could only get one week off, so I'm joining them halfway through.'

'And Barbara usually packs for both of you, I see,' said Imogen, unpacking the sandwiches, and pouring juice. Mike picked up both halves of his sandwich at once and consumed it hungrily. Luckily Imogen had bought two packs for him. When she got to the iron she saw at once what was wrong. It had run out of water and was set at high heat for steam.

'Shall I show you how to use this, or shall I just do it for you?' she asked.

'Each to his own trade,' said Mike, grinning. 'You iron; I'll dispense this urgently needed advice. What have you done? Murdered a don? Your obvious defence is provocation.'

'No. Sorry. My hands are clean of scholarly blood. I am not provoked.'

'You must have the patience of a saint to be unprovoked by that lot!' he said, throwing a sweater into the case on top of the shoes. 'Seriously, nurse, what's up?'

'It's a missing person,' said Imogen. 'Nobody I know. But I would dearly like to know more about the circumstances in which they disappeared. And about what enquiries were made and such.'

'On our patch? A Cambridge person?'

'Don't know. Have no special reason to think so. All I know is her name. Is there a register?'

'Scotland Yard keep one. You're supposed to be able to match details of DBs with descriptions of missing persons. It doesn't by any means always work.'

'DBs?'

'Dead Bodies – when you've found one with absolutely nothing on them to identify them.'

'If someone just disappears from their house . . .'

'Well, it isn't necessarily a police matter. It's not against the law to do a bunk, if you don't leave unpaid debts or whatever. The Sally Army are quite good at tracing people. You could try them. But why are you interested? What's the handle?'

'It's what she was working on. She was called May Swann, and she was writing a biography of a fellow of the college. She just disappeared.'

'Boredom?'

'That might be nearer than you think!' said Imogen laughing. 'But the papers seem to have been retrieved from her abandoned dwelling, and passed to another biographer. He died, rather suddenly.'

'What of? Any hint of foul play?'

'I don't *think* so. Seems to have been meningitis.'

'But my thriller-reading friend has spotted a coincidence. I see.'

'It is a coincidence.'

'Yes. Slightly. When did she vanish?'

'I don't know exactly. About eighteen months ago would be my guess. What sort of things could I find out from this Scotland Yard register?'

'Absolutely zilch. It's all regarded as confidential and you aren't next of kin, or even best pal. I'll have to do it for you.'

'When you get back then . . .'

'No time like the present. I'll phone them. You just keep ironing!'

He went through to the hallway, and closed the door behind him. Imogen ironed two more shirts, folded them neatly and then looked despairingly at the chaotic suitcase. Mike's voice could be heard faintly through the door. 'Yes, I'm holding . . .'

Imogen tipped the contents of the case out on to the sofa, and started again.

'This is what I've got,' said Mike reappearing. He had a notepad in his hand and was reading from it. '"Aged forty-one. Lived at 13, Beachcroft Road, Edmonton. Last seen 22nd March, 1992, by land-lady. Reported missing by nephew, David Swann, 15th April, 1992. No sightings. No unidentified DBs match description. Case remains on file." Here. Have it for what it's worth.' Mike tore the sheet from the notepad and handed it to her. Then his eyes lit on the suitcase.

'Bloody hell, Imogen – how is Barbara to believe I packed that? She'll think I've had another woman here!'

'Well, you have, haven't you? Give her my good wishes, and have a lovely time,' said Imogen, putting on her coat, and folding the sheet of paper into her bag.

Directory enquiries found seven David Swanns. It's one of the benefits of the new customer aware system that they can look for a name nationwide if you haven't a clue about an address. They were all over the place, from Peebles to Finchley. Imogen tried the Peebles one first, bearing in mind the longish interval between the disappearance and the nephew reporting it. The most likely explanation was that he lived far off, and didn't visit often. The Peebles David Swann denied all knowledge of any May Swann. He was rather curt about it. So were the next four. But Imogen allowed for the fact that she was in fact being cheeky in telephoning out of the blue like that. It was called "cold calling" she remembered, when indulged in by double-glazing sales staff. And at least they had something to offer. It was theoretically possible that one wanted their dreadful windows. She must try to be civil next time they called her. She made herself a cup of coffee before trying the Finchley number. Suddenly her luck changed.

'Oh, yes!' the voice on the phone said. A woman's voice. 'That's David's aunt. You don't have news of her, do you?'

'I'm afraid not,' said Imogen. 'I work at St Agatha's College, Cambridge. Summerfield was a fellow here, and I am trying to sort out the progress of his biography. I wondered if anyone in May Swann's family could cast any light.' She had a slight pang of conscience at giving a misleading impression. But she hadn't actually told a lie – she did work at St Agatha's, and Summerfield had been a fellow there.

'You could come and talk to David,' said the voice. 'But I don't think he can help. He did everything possible at the time. It was perfectly horrid.'

'I'm sure it was,' said Imogen.' Would he mind talking to me?'

'I don't think so,' said the voice. 'He doesn't get in till eight most evenings, though, and then he needs his supper.'

'What about Saturday? Could I try Saturday?' Fran was away for the weekend, and Imogen had two blank days in her diary.

'Fine. Come in the afternoon – my mother takes the children out, and there might be a little peace and quiet.'

'Splendid. Next Saturday, around three?'

'Who shall I say it is?'

'Imogen Quy. Q-U-Y, rhymes with "why".'

'Like Quy near Cambridge,' the voice said. 'I'm Emily Swann. I'll tell David to expect you.'

The Swanns lived in a thirties semi, in a quiet street off North Finchley High Road. Emily Swann had made tea. There were toys scattered everywhere, and a battered appearance to the furniture, but the house was bright and cheerful. David Swann was a tall gangling man of rather harassed appearance. He led Imogen into the front room, where she spotted files on his desk, labelled 'Marshall and Swann, Accountants'. He asked her to sit down.

'Now, what is all this about?' he asked.

'We are trying to find out all we can about the progress of the proposed biography of Gideon Summerfield. And we understand that your aunt was working on it at the time of her disappearance,' said Imogen. 'We wondered if there was any connection between her work and . . .'

'If there was, I wouldn't know about it,' said David Swann. 'She didn't confide in me.'

Imogen paused, waiting.

'I didn't get on with her at all,' he said. 'I paid duty calls from time to time, since I was her last living relative. But she didn't have a lot of time for accountants. She thought they were money-grubbers – prey to greed. I thought that was pretty silly, not to say offensive. But I once remarked that her devoted scholarship was remarkably badly paid, and she never forgave me.'

'So you didn't know she was working on Summerfield?'

'Well, as a matter of fact I did. She thought because I could do accounts, and he was a mathematician, I would understand his work, and could explain it to her. I said I would try – would have given us something to talk about when I went over to see her. But the stuff was geometry – absolutely bugger all to do with accounts, believe me. So I said sorry, no can do, and she offered to pay me for my efforts.'

'Having concluded that your inability to help her was occasioned by . . .'

'My general lack of interest in anything but money. Exactly. I was seriously annoyed – to put it mildly, and so I didn't get over there for a couple of months. When I did she had gone.'

'Taking the work she was doing?'

'Oh, no, taking not a thing, as far as I could see, and leaving two weeks rent unpaid. Nearly all her clothes were there, and her cheque book, but she had drawn two hundred and fifty pounds the day before she left, and taken a weekend case. She told the landlady she would be gone for a few days, but she didn't say where she was going.'

'If this trip of hers was connected with the biography in any way, it might have been possible by looking at her files, to work out where she had gone . . .'

'I thought so too. But the publishers had taken the files before I got there. They said when she reappeared she could get in touch, but time pressure was so great that they reserved the right to get someone else to complete the book. That's what really convinced me to report it to the police, and start a search for her. She was a crazy old bat, if you'll forgive my language, Miss Quy, but she did care about her work.'

'Had she done other biographies?'

'Several. We've got copies somewhere. Haven't read them myself. They're all about such boring people. Now if she had done a golfer, or a jazz player . . . As you see, I can't help you.'

'You are helping. Do you know how far your aunt had got with the book?'

'She'd been working on it for months. I'm not sure exactly. She always did work for ages for very little pay. You couldn't calculate her hourly rate unless you could do small fractions. It was stupid. It was just so she could call herself a writer, or a biographer or something. She could type, and file things. She could have got a nice little office job, and been quite comfortable. But no, not her!'

'And you never saw any of her work on Summerfield?'

'Well, yes, I *saw* it – it was always lying round on every table and shelf in her flat, but I didn't read it – only the monograph by the man himself that she wanted me to expound to her.'

'Mr Swann, what do you think has become of your aunt?'

'I think she's come to harm, Miss Quy. I think she's stepped under a bus in Manchester, or been murdered by a pickpocket, or slipped into a river and drowned, or lost her memory and been confined to a hospital . . . It just isn't – wasn't – like her to leave unfinished work. And come to that it wasn't like her to leave her rent unsettled. She wouldn't have gone off and done that. Of course she might have known I would settle it for her . . . but it wasn't like her. You know, Miss Quy, when people are hard up they are sometimes very particular about money . . . she was like that. The police agreed with me, when they got the picture. They put out an alert, and a description. I think they're still trying to find her. But they haven't succeeded.'

7

Why would someone just walk out on a book in progress? Boredom? It would have to be very lethal boredom to make one abandon one's whole lifestyle, and simply flee. Imogen resolved to ask Fran just *how* boring Summerfield had been. But meanwhile she cooked up another ruse, carefully designing it as she drove home. It would have to wait till Monday, of course.

And when she got in the little light on her answerphone was blipping furiously, and she found something else to worry her. The Master's secretary had been phoning at half-hour intervals all afternoon. The last message on the tape was from Lady B. It said simply, 'Please get in touch as soon as you return. Don't wait till Monday.' Imogen, out of an instinct for self-preservation, put on the kettle, and put her slice of quiche in the oven to warm before phoning the Master's Lodge.

'Trouble, I'm afraid,' said Lady B. 'One of our young men has been accused of cheating in the Tripos exam. Very mediocre student; very brilliant essay.'

'Who is it?' asked Imogen.

'Bob Framingham. Philosophy.'

'Oh, yes. I think I do know him . . .'

'He has an excuse – or an explanation, rather, Imogen. He says you gave him medication which made him exceptionally lucid and fluent.'

'I did?' Imogen was momentarily stunned.

'That's what he says. He says it accounts for his unusually good performance.'

'Well, I can't have given him anything much at all, if he came to me just before an exam. I might dole out two paracetamol to help someone calm down and sleep well the night before; otherwise I send them to the doctor.'

'Always?'

'Always.'

'I think he's going to be very obstinate and difficult, Imogen. He's getting a lawyer.'

'If I gave him even paracetamol it will be in the book.'

'Of course – you keep a book . . .'

'With everything in it. Dose, time of day, reason for giving it . . . We have to be preternaturally careful . . .'

'We?'

'College nurses. If we make mistakes our colleges are liable. As a matter of fact, someone who needs paracetamol is more likely to ask a friend for some, or skid over to Boots; it's less trouble.'

'Does paracetamol put a sudden intellectual shine on people?'

'Not that I ever heard. In fact a major reason for being so careful, and sending them off to the doctor at exam times is the very opposite – the risk of being blamed for a poor performance. I would have done better, but nurse doped me – that sort of thing.'

'The Senior Tutor is dealing with it. Could you let him have a copy of the entry in your book as soon as possible? And, Imogen – I'm sorry about this.'

'Not your fault, is it?' said Imogen reasonably. 'I'll zip over to college tomorrow and copy the relevant page of the book.'

'When you do, pop in and have a word with John Spandrel, will you?' said Lady B. 'As Senior Tutor he's in charge of this can of worms.'

'I thought you'd better know what's going on, Imogen,' said John Spandrel. 'Have a sherry?' He waved her towards an armchair at his fireside. His room was dark and ancient, and furnished with heavy large couch and chairs. The walls were covered with prints of the college at various times of its life, and prints of Roman piazzas, and wild Tuscan landscapes. It was loud with the ticking of an immense grandfather clock, decorated by angels and signs of the zodiac, that stood under a massive ceiling beam in the darkest corner. He proffered sherry in a delicately engraved glass with a spiral stem that looked rather too good to use.

'Thank you, John,' said Imogen. 'Now what has this villain been up to?'

'It looks like a very clear case of cheating,' John Spandrel said. 'Framingham has very modest abilities, in the normal course of events. He has produced a philosophy essay in the Tripos which though not word for word throughout is remarkably like the essay of another examinee. To cap it all, both essays are remarkably like an essay submitted for the Random Memorial Prize by a third undergraduate. The other two aren't ours – one's at Pembroke, and the other at Girton.'

'Fill me in, John, – I don't know what the Random Prize is.'

'For an essay on a topic in philosophy. It's conducted rather like an exam – aspirants have to present themselves on the appointed morning, and write it on the spot. It's got considerable cachet, and it carries a bursary of seven hundred pounds. Well worth winning, in fact.'

'Is it set before the date of the Tripos exam?'

'A full month before. This year's winner was a chap called Melvin Luffincott. It's his essay that has cropped up in these other papers. It's a sheer fluke that the full extent of the wickedness was noticed; but it just happens that the assessors for the Random Prize included one of the Tripos examiners. Usually the same people don't mark both, to spread the workload round the faculty; this year someone fell ill suddenly, and Peter Prestwick did both jobs. Of course he spotted at once that there was something fishy, and raised a hue and cry. Then one of the other examiners realised one of his papers was very like . . . To cap it all, our young dolt, who says that your pills made him unduly brilliant, had folded his paper in four. He says he finished early, and just folded the paper up in boredom . . . then he flattened it out and handed it in. I ask you!'

'I don't quite follow this . . .' said Imogen.

'Well, you'd be surprised how often fishy papers turn out to have been folded or crumpled. It's nearly impossible to smuggle ready-written stuff into the exam room still pristine and flat.'

'I see. And what do the other two people involved say?'

'The Girton chap says he has no explanation; no idea how it happened. His paper was flat – and he wasn't sitting directly beside Framingham. But he does know him well. He says they belong to a discussion group which Luffincott also belongs to. And Luffincott professes himself outraged, and hotly denies having given any help, or any copy of his essay to either of them.'

'Would this Luffincott have a copy? If he had written the essay under supervision, and handed it in?'

'Well, a prize competition isn't exactly like an examination, Imogen, and a significant difference is that when the judging is over, the candidates are given their entries back.'

'And they were given them back . . .'

'Three days before the Tripos.'

'I don't envy you having to sort it all out, John.'

'I don't have to, thank God. It's a university matter, not a college one. There'll be a Court of Discipline.'

'What's that?'

'It consists of a group of lawyers, and lay senior members. They will hear the case. Framingham has the right to be represented. His tutor offers to act on his behalf, and represent him; but Framingham has declined the offer, and will have a lawyer of his own choosing. That lets Emlyn Bent off the hook, anyway. It takes a lawyer's training to be energetic in the defence of someone one thinks guilty as charged. However, the college isn't out of the woods entirely – the Court of Discipline is bound to want to take evidence from you, in view of this farrago about pills.'

'I see.'

'Imogen, we – the College Council I mean – are somewhat alarmed. We don't seem to know whether you can be compelled to attend such a hearing. It being nothing to do with the law of the land, and the days of the Star Chamber being long past.'

'That doesn't arise. I shan't refuse to attend. I would look on it as an extension of the job for which the college pays me.'

'It isn't likely to be much fun. There will be a skilled and forceful attempt to suggest that you gave inappropriate medication. We think the college should pay for you to have legal advice of your own.'

'Forgive me, John, but I don't agree. It is a very simple matter in so far as it concerns me. I kept a record in my book. I am sure I didn't give any drug capable of having the effect suggested, and I can say so if asked. Having a lawyer of my own looks over-defensive to me; as if I thought I had done something that put me in need of defending.'

'Hmm. Do think it over, Imogen. What would you say, for example, if someone suggested you might have given out something which is not in the book, and simply forgotten? The college will employ a lawyer for you. You have only to ask.'

'I really wouldn't have done that,' said Imogen. 'That would be a major dereliction of duty, which I could not possibly have perpetrated. But all right, I'll think it over and let you know.'

All that was a fairly powerful distraction from thoughts of May Swann. And Fran did not appear on Sunday evening, so that Imogen still had not spoken to her on Monday morning, when she telephoned

Recktype and Diss, with a disingenuous query. She asked for an editor in charge of biography, and was put through to one Angela Kingsweir.

'I wonder if you can help me?' she asked. 'I am trying to make contact with an old friend, and I believe she was working on a biography of Gideon Summerfield . . .'

'May Swann?' said the voice.

'Yes!' said Imogen brightly. 'Do you have her address?'

'No, we don't,' said Ms Kingsweir. 'I'm afraid we can't help you.'

'But the biography . . .'

'Miss Swann abandoned it. She did not see fit to tell us, let alone to tell us why, or to give us a forwarding address. We have been put to considerable trouble and expense, and the first half of the advance is still outstanding. We would dearly like to communicate with the lady ourselves.'

'Oh,' said Imogen. 'How distressing; and how odd. Really it isn't at all like her . . . Do you think she's all right?'

'I honestly wouldn't know,' said the voice. 'But I know this project is jinxed. And she wouldn't be the first author to scarper with an advance, I can tell you.'

'What did you mean about the project being jinxed?' asked Imogen.

'It's been endless trouble. For one thing, you can't imagine how difficult it was to recover the papers from May Swann's lodgings. We had to brief a lawyer . . . The literary executor was going bananas about it.'

'Papers?' said Imogen, acting dumb.

'Relating to the life of Summerfield. They are the property of his executors. Miss Swann was lent them in good faith on the assumption that she would make legitimate use of them and return them.'

'Executors?' said Imogen.

'Of Summerfield's literary estate. Without which, of course, no other biographer can proceed. Your old friend simply left them behind her when she bunked off with the money.'

'Oh, but I'm sure she wouldn't have . . .'

'Authors,' said the voice, 'are so unreliable.'

Imogen next saw Fran on Monday evening. Fran came bouncing in, announced that she was jolly hungry, and had forgotten to shop, and could she do anything to help with supper . . . Imogen invited her, laughing, and got her to set the table while she concocted a curry.

Once they were sitting comfortably at the table in the little breakfast room, Imogen asked her how the great work was going.

'Well, I haven't started to write it yet. So in one way I don't know. I just might find myself incapable of getting words on paper, like my friend Mitchell.'

'Whyever would you find yourself incapable of getting words on paper? Haven't you been writing essays these many years? And who's Mitchell?'

'He's a friend. Or rather, a friend of Josh's. His father is fairly filthy rich, and Mitch wants to be a novelist, so father is paying for him to stay on in Cambridge and work on a book. Mitch is very bright, and he's got lots of ideas. But somehow he can't get started. He's always doing research, or making notes. I might be like him.'

'You might not be. I would blame his father. If the fellow had to get a job it would concentrate his mind.'

'It isn't like you to be unkind, Imogen,' said Fran.

'Is "unkind" current jargon for "spot on"?' said Imogen, crisply. 'So: you haven't started to write yet . . .'

'But I've got a fairly good grip on all this paperwork now. There's just one gap – I need to find out where he spent the summer of '78. Then the tally of his days is complete, and I can get writing.'

'And Mark Zephyr's notes don't cast any light?'

'Nope. Nobody seems to have got that bit.'

'Neither Zephyr nor Swann?'

Fran looked at Imogen strangely. Then she started to say something, and stopped. Instead she said, 'Pass the mango chutney, would you?'

'It turns out that Mark Zephyr was the brother of a friend of mine,' said Imogen, passing the chutney jar. 'He died suddenly of meningitis, poor fellow. But while he was going strong he had a little difficulty with Janet Summerfield. And he wasn't the first on the job. May Swann was working on it before him, as we thought. Remember, you asked me where she was now?'

'It's a good question. I don't suppose we shall ever know.'

'You could be right. I've been ferreting around. She disappeared. Taking an advance from Recktype and Diss, and leaving all the documents from the Summerfield estate in her lodging. Everyone says it wasn't at all like her, except her publishers who reckon that authors are capable of anything.'

'Exactly why have you been ferreting, Imogen?' said Fran.

'Friendly interest.'

'In me?'

'Well, not in Summerfield, anyway. Do you mind?'

'I'm not sure. You'd better tell me about it.'

Imogen recounted the gist of her conversation with Pamela Zephyr, and with David Swann. They had finished eating, and were clearing dishes when she got to the end of the story.

'Great!' said Fran drily. 'Just great. And what happened to Ian Goliard?'

'Who?'

'The fellow who was working on this book before May Swann.'

'God, Fran – was there?'

'There certainly was. Unmistakable traces. Once one gets everything sorted there it is. Three previous folk. All stopped in midstream.'

'That's a hefty, nasty coincidence . . . It must be coincidence. Or, at least Mark Zephyr must be. You couldn't catch meningitis from a stack of papers. I am very sure of that.'

'It's a bigger coincidence than it looks, actually,' said Fran. 'All three of these projects were interrupted at the same point. Or on the same point of enquiry, rather.'

'I don't understand you . . .'

'When, for one reason or another, each of these three stopped work, they were at the point of wondering where the great Summerfield was during the summer of 1978. Ian Goliard hadn't got very far. He had made a sort of calendar, tracing Summerfield's movements from birth, through school and college, and addresses and holidays. It's quite a neat idea, really. I suppose he intended to go on to attach information and documents to each place in turn. Anyway his calendar is quite full and detailed as far as spring '78, and then stops with "August – away??" '

'Fran, how do you know this was someone called Goliard and not May Swann or Mark Zephyr?'

'Different paper; different method of work; different handwriting . . .'

'Yes, I see.'

'And in any case he put his name in tiny letters on the bottom left-hand corner of each sheet of paper in his files. There might have been more, of course, not kept by his successors. But the calendar is there, has his name on it, and is very full and complete as far as it goes.'

'And it goes until . . .'

'August '78. Summerfield went on holiday. He and his wife rented a cottage in the Malverns. Or so the calendar says. They took the cottage for a month, and various of their friends came and went, joining them for days at a time. At some stage there was a quarrel and Summerfield went off for a few days – somewhere, we wot not where.'

'Alone?'

'Perhaps not; but I don't know who with. The rest is silence. From Goliard, anyway.'

'So he gave up on the project, and it was handed to May Swann?'

'That's what it looks like. She was very systematic. As you know, she assigned numbers to all the original papers she had been given. She copied Goliard's calendar headings into a notebook, putting the dates and places as headings, and listing all the material on that place and time that she had been able to find. She went past summer '78; she took the method right through to Summerfield's death. There is something on nearly every page – even if it's only business letters, or an announcement of a lecture series he was giving in a certain term. In a separate notebook she began drafting the actual text of the book.'

'But she had got well past August '78?'

'Only in a way. August '78 headed a blank page. She had *something* however slight, on every other page from birth to death.'

'But you don't know if she was trying to fill in that particular blank when she disappeared?' Imogen was clutching at straws.

'Oh yes, I do.' Fran was almost gleeful. 'She was under time pressure. She kept a work diary. She roughed out the week's work for herself every Monday, estimating the time that the next chunks of work would take. Her last work diary entry says "Find out about August '78." It's heavily underlined. And dated 20th March, two days before she vanished.'

'Fran . . .'

'You're going to ask about Zephyr. Well, I'm only guessing. He took over May Swann's research work, and just set about checking and ordering it. I imagine he found she was reliable, and decided to accept her version of events, and simply write it up.'

'But he couldn't accept her version of this holiday in '78 . . .'

'Because there wasn't one. Exactly. And didn't you tell me that his sister said he had just one little matter to find out about and then it would be ready to write? Something like that?'

'Yes,' said Imogen. 'She did say something like that.'

'Well, what's the betting that one little thing will turn out to be August '78?'

'We can ask Pamela that,' said Imogen.

But Pamela, consulted on the phone while Fran cleared the table, could not remember.

8

'You wouldn't feel like lending me the car?' Fran asked the next morning. 'I'll need it all day.'

'Today? That's all right. I need it myself tomorrow,' said Imogen, abstractedly. She was eating toast and reading the *Independent*.

'Thanks,' said Fran. 'It's a pig of a journey otherwise.'

'Where's that?' asked Imogen. She was somewhat sleepy, the conversation about coincidence the night before having turned philosophical, and gone on rather late.

'Castle Acre. I might not be back by supper time. I'll buy the car some petrol.'

'You're welcome. Have you decided what to do about the missing summer of Summerfield?'

'Yes. Ask. What else could I do?'

'Forget it. Fudge. Simply leave it out . . .'

'You know me better than that.'

'Who could you ask?'

'Janet Summerfield. That's what I want the car for. She lives at Castle Acre, and she's not in the phone book. I'll have to go on spec.'

'From all accounts, you'll get your head bitten off,' said Imogen. 'Are you sure you've got to accost her?'

'Quite sure. Even if she didn't herself go on this blasted escape trip, she presumably knows where *he* went.'

'Fran, you must have realised that you yourself are now precisely at the point . . .'

'Which defeated all the others? Quite a challenge, isn't it?'

'Well . . .' Imogen bit back the over-anxious and certainly counter-productive 'Take care . . .' and replaced it with 'Drive carefully'. Since it was her car, she was entitled to say that.

On her way into college, later in the morning, Imogen saw that the Clare College Fellows' garden was open, and she turned into it to take a look at the autumn colours – trees on the river bank, the autumn crocus palely loitering in the grass, and the Michaelmas daisies in the borders. One of the benefits of Imogen's life-style was leisure. She worked part-time for St Agatha's College. Once she had had a portfolio of jobs, adding up to more than full-time, and had had no time to enjoy the money she earned. Then she realised that leisure was the most luxurious thing money could buy. She resigned from every college but her favourite one. Now, like most part-time workers, she put in many more hours than she was paid for, but even so she had privileges to offset against the need for thrift. She could set her own working hours, and take time for shopping, wandering and thinking.

This fine crisp autumn day, for example, she had allowed time for some filing and tidying in her office before her official surgery hour, and could on impulse decide to spend the time instead staring at the butter-yellow leaves of the sunlit flowering cherry trees, some hanging on to their branches, and others lying in a golden disc beneath them on the grass. She tried to imagine what fabrics might achieve that bright cool contrast in a quilt. It was just warm enough in the sun to sit for a few moments on a damp bench, and relish the day. The garden competed with her background anxiety about Fran. Of course it was possible that something about Mark Zephyr had irritated Janet Summerfield, and would explain, if one had known him, why she had harassed him. Not that she had harassed him to the end – hadn't Pamela said that he had come back pleased from his encounter with her the day he fell ill? And Imogen found it hard to imagine a person in their right mind not taking to Fran. You can give reasons why some people are immediately likeable – you can use words like candour, cheerfulness, warm-heartedness . . . but in the end it's a mystery. Nor, thought Imogen, do we have any way of acknowledging these forms of liking, these gentler kinds of love. 'Friendship' is supposed to cover all.

And what a narrow stereotype of friendship people have! The word wouldn't suggest an anxious landlady – and someone considerably older. Fear for Fran, sharp concern for her safety and prosperity was *ultra vires* from Imogen. She sighed. A shadow fell across her, and she looked up to see Lady Buckmote looking down at her.

'You look thoughtful, Imogen,' said Lady B. 'I hope this cheating uproar isn't worrying you.'

'No, no,' said Imogen getting up. 'Something quite other. I'm sorry; it seems a sin to gloom at these lovely trees.'

'It does rather. Are you on your way in to college? Shall we walk together?'

'Let's.'

'I've got some news,' said Lady B., as they crossed the Clare College bridge, with its prettily sagging parapet, and marble balls poised atop it. 'The college powers have offered a fellowship to Dr Maverack.'

'Really?' Imogen sounded as she felt, surprised. 'I thought the feeling was flowing rather against.'

'Well, nobody was very keen. But a worse prospect was looming. You know that colleges are supposed to take in these wandering scholars roughly fairly – shared out so to speak. The fair shares system only arises when someone isn't welcome – often there's hot competition to get someone.'

'But not for Maverack?'

'Indeed not. Only news came on the grape vine that the *next* homeless eminence would be Hugo Obverse – and the thought of *him* is so horrible that the college snapped up Maverack at once. We couldn't be expected to take two googlies in a row, you see.'

'So taking Maverack is a sort of protection racket?' said Imogen, laughing. 'How does everyone know that Obverse would be even worse?'

'No contest,' said Lady B. 'Obverse is notorious throughout the English speaking world.'

'What for?' asked Imogen. So Lady B. regaled her with stories of the horrible Hugo all the way to the college gates. What hadn't this monster of academe perpetrated? Seducing his students – of both sexes – quarrelling with colleagues, getting drunk at high tables, delivering lectures in alcoholic stupors, losing examination scripts, hacking into colleagues' computers and leaving obscene jokes on the screens, getting his air fares to the States paid four times over by four different Mid Western universities, and then not turning up to give the promised lectures at any of them . . .

'But why isn't he cast out into exterior darkness?' asked Imogen. 'Why does anyone want him in Cambridge? How does he get away with it?'

'He's brilliant. A world-class intellect. And Cambridge is about intellect, not niceness. However, fear not. We will put up with Maverack, and someone else will have to suffer Obverse.'

'But Maverack is long-winded,' said Imogen, 'and Obverse . . .'

'At least sounds interesting? I fear it would pall quickly in the event.'

Hugo Obverse however, thought Imogen, as she walked across the court to her office, having taken her leave of Lady B., sounded like a whole lot more fun for a biographer than Gideon Summerfield, whose wild oats had left no traces, and been confined to a single summer well into his middle age.

Naturally Imogen was on tenterhooks for Fran's return. Anxiety was making her slightly trembly. The moment she heard the front door she trotted into the hall, where Fran was hanging her jacket on the hall stand, and said, 'How did it go?'

'Very mixed,' said Fran. 'Have you got any tonic, Imogen? I've got a smidgen of gin left, and I need a drink!'

'Tonic no. Bitter lemon, yes. Or you could have some whisky.'

'I'll go and get my gin, thanks. Tell you all about it in a mo.'

Imogen emphatically didn't feel like cooking supper. She laid out salad, and bread and cheese, and sliced ham from the deli on the corner, and a jar of home-made pickle.

'Very basic supper,' she said, when Fran reappeared, 'but you'll eat with me, will you?' She didn't herself feel very hungry.

'Swap,' said Fran. 'A tot of my gin for you, and a supper from your supplies for me.'

'Done,' said Imogen. 'Now tell me.'

'I spent the morning hanging about. She wasn't in, and her neighbours said she usually went shopping in King's Lynn on a Tuesday morning. I looked round the village – it's very pretty. Big church one end, Norman castle the other. There's a good pub. I had a coffee, and lurked around. She's got a small, very bijou Georgian cottage on the green. By and by she came home.'

'What's she like?'

'Sort of – ample. Blue rinsed. Wearing velvet and Morrissy prints. Like a ship in full sail.'

Imogen smiled. 'And were you welcome?'

'At first, yes. I helped carry the shopping bags in from the car – she has asthma, and she was a bit breathless. Then she got uptight when she realised what I was after.'

'Didn't you tell her right away? What did you say?'

'At first I just said I was at Cambridge and interested in her husband's work,' said Fran. 'So she thought I was a mathematician.

Then when we'd got the shopping all stowed she made a cup of tea, and sat me in the living-room, and I explained a bit more, and she was very disconabulated.'

'Discombobulated, you mean, dear child.'

'Whatever. She obviously didn't know that Professor Maverack had farmed out the work on the biography, and I had to cover my tracks, or his tracks, rather, quickly, and say that I was his student doing a bit of preparatory work for him, and try to unmention that I was doing it all.'

'Hmm. Awkward . . .'

'Very. But then she got very friendly and helpful, and fetched out an album of family photos to show me. She said she had lent a lot of family papers, she understood they were with Professor Maverack at the moment, and they included all the loose photographs, but she had held on to the albums, as she hadn't wanted to unstick the mounted photographs. So we spent a little while looking at all these pics together. We might have been old pals. Of course I kept hoping one of the little captions would say "Summer '78". No such luck. And I kept putting my foot in it by failing to recognise her in the snaps.'

'Little blurry black and white things, about the size of a postage stamp?' said Imogen, taking her empty glass through to the kitchen, and returning to invite Fran to sit opposite her at the table.

'Partly that. And partly she kept changing. I mean, the woman sitting on more than half the sofa with me just didn't look like the slender one in a swimsuit standing on a beach in Brittany in 1955.'

'*Eheu, fugaces!*' said Imogen learnedly. 'Few of us do look like ourselves as time goes by.'

'Yes, but . . .'

'But what?' asked Imogen.

'She had done it more than once. She had kept doing it.'

'Doing what?'

'Changing. Putting on weight and losing it again. I mean, only the very young ones showed her looking slender. After that she varied between being on the plump side of normal, and being absolutely massive – like a Michelin woman. She was telling me who the people in the snapshots were, and I asked, "And who's that?" and she got a bit shirty. She said, "That's me," as though I were a half wit, but honestly she wasn't recognisable from one to another. The state she is in now is a kind of compromise between extremes.'

'And was there a photo of summer '78?'

'No. So eventually I asked her about it. And she went berserk.'

'What do you mean? Tell me more.'

'She started yelling. She said . . . Well, to tell the truth I was so startled that I'm not sure I can remember her very words, but the gist of it was that she had told people over and over again that it didn't matter, to leave it out, to just get on with the job and forget about it and it had no significance, and nobody would take any notice of her as though she had no rights, and her opinion didn't matter a damn when actually she obviously knew everything there was to know about poor Gideon, having spent every waking minute of her life completely dedicated to him, and if she said it didn't matter where he went one summer, what insolent overmighty person could dare to say it did . . . on and on. I jumped up off the sofa and backed away from her.'

'Not surprising. Golly, Fran.'

'Then she really got warmed up. About how the papers were hers, and the biography couldn't be written without her consent, and she would jolly well see to it that the matter was omitted, or the book would get vetoed, she'd get an injunction. She was bitterly disappointed in Dr Maverack, she had been promised he was a man of discretion, and she thought he had understood the biography was to chart the career of a great modern thinker, and not to go muck-raking around among the trivia of his private life . . . just on and on. Then she threw me out.'

'Not laying hands on you?'

'Oh, no. I didn't wait to see if she would. I just grabbed my jacket and notebook and ran. She followed me down the garden path, fist clenched and shouting the same things over and over.'

'She sounds completely potty. Pamela said she was deranged.'

'Well, maybe . . .' Fran sounded doubtful. 'You know, Imogen, I'm not sure. It sounds potty when I tell you about it, but at the time . . .'

'You can't have felt she was entirely normal, surely?'

'Of course not. And yet this uproar didn't feel exactly *mad*, all the same. She seemed more malevolent than out of control. I can't explain it properly. It didn't feel so much like being the butt of a crazy outburst, just random, like a gust of wind in someone's mind; it felt more deliberate. She meant to cow me. She turned it on like a kitchen tap, somehow.'

'So what do you conclude?'

'Well, I shall have to tell Professor Maverack about it first thing tomorrow. And hope to get to him with my version before she gets there with hers. And also, it is of the first importance to discover what it is about that holiday . . . Nothing on earth will prevent me trying to crack it.'

'Fran, we might be melodramatising coincidence. But you have realised that it seems unlucky – perhaps even dangerous, to pursue that?'

'Imogen, *what is this*?' cried Fran. 'What *could* the old bore have done on holiday? And all that time ago?'

'Robbed a bank?' offered Imogen. 'Fathered a child?'

'You haven't eaten anything, hardly,' said Fran suddenly. 'Are you all right?'

'I feel a bit wobbly, to tell the truth,' said Imogen. 'I might go straight to bed.'

'Haha,' said Fran. '*I* get to look after *you*, at last. The tenant's revenge. Off you go then, and I'll bring you a hot-water bottle.'

9

Flu is horrible. Luckily one forgets from one attack to another how nasty it is, or anyone like Imogen who mixes with a lot of people and is exposed to germs would be in perpetual dread of catching it. Next morning, feeling spectacularly feverish and aching from top to toe, Imogen kept to her bed. Fran seemed more pleased at her opportunity to reciprocate kindness than sorry for Imogen's misery, but she brought breakfast in bed for the sufferer – toast and Marmite and French-style milky white coffee – and then removed the tray and produced a damp towel made piping hot in the microwave, so that Imogen could freshen up without getting up. Then, sitting in the little bright blue basket-weave armchair that occupied the corner of Imogen's bedroom, she asked, 'Will you be all right if I leave you for a bit?'

'Fine. I'll just sleep it off.'

'Only I really need to catch Dr Maverack – Professor Maverack, I mean, this morning and have a few things out with him.'

'I'll be fine. Good luck bearding the lion in his den . . .' Imogen was half asleep before the sentence was finished.

She was woken by an aggressive hammering on her front door. Someone was not only bashing the Victorian iron knocker, but whacking the door with the flat of the hand. Not a chance that anyone knocking like that would give up and go away easily. Whatever was going on? Was her chimney on fire? Of course not – Imogen got herself sitting up, and put her feet into her slippers. She got herself unsteadily across the room, took her dressing-gown off the hook, and put it on. The beating on the door continued. Moving slowly, feeling light-headed, and with her knees aching, Imogen got herself downstairs. Somehow the racket at the door felt daunting in her fragile state, and she went instead to the living-room, where the bay window let her see through the swathes of net curtain that conferred privacy to the room, who was standing on her little front garden path.

A man was knocking. A woman in a dark coat was standing behind him. Both were strangers. Imogen proceeded slowly and reluctantly to her door.

'Who is it?' she called.

'Open up, please,' said the voice, peremptorily.

Imogen put the door on the chain, and opened it a crack. The moment she did so the person outside tried to thrust it open, and step in. The chain was taut.

'Who are you and what do you want?' asked Imogen. The flu gave her voice a·quavering tone, and sapped her authority.

'Is this the residence of one Frances Bullion?' enquired the woman.

'Yes. She is not at home.'

'We do not require to see her. She has in her possession certain documents which are my property,' said the woman. 'We have come to retrieve them. Please let us in and show us which parts of the premises are occupied by Miss Bullion, so that we can find what we have come for as quickly as possible.'

'Let you search Miss Bullion's flat in her absence and take things away?' said Imogen. 'Certainly not. Please go away.'

'I am entitled to recover my property,' said the woman. This must, of course, Imogen realised, be Janet Summerfield.

'This house is *my* property,' she retorted. 'And you are not entitled to enter it without my consent.'

'It's a cheap and lightweight chain,' said the man. 'I can break it easily.'

'Forcible entry is a criminal offence,' said Imogen. 'As also is the assault you would need to commit to get past me in this narrow hallway if I stood my ground. And I will stand my ground. If you have lawful business with Miss Bullion you must pursue it in lawful ways.'

Janet Summerfield suddenly offered a grimace, which might have been a placatory smile. 'Look, there's no need for this,' she said. 'It's all very simple, and there's no need at all to involve landladies. Miss Bullion has been lent some documents of mine. I require them to be returned. I can easily identify them. It would not involve ransacking the place, or breaking locks. Just picking up a few papers . . .'

'You may be able to identify them,' said Imogen coldly. 'But I can't. I don't know what is yours and what is Miss Bullion's. I cannot allow the removal from her flat of anything at all. Please leave.'

The cold draught from the partly open door was cutting round Imogen's ankles. She was beginning to shake – standing in the cold with a high temperature not being a good idea – and she was a little frightened. Janet Summerfield was brimming with hostility, and a sort of self-righteous rage. Her unidentified companion was beefy, with a thick fist, clenched round the door chain, and a stupid expression. Wherever had she got him from?

And then, suddenly, Imogen was rescued. From the street behind the visitors a voice hailed her. 'Everything all right, Miss Quy?' There was Josh, and Simon, who had been her lodger last year, with two friends. They were young, and athletic looking, and one of the friends was nearly as bulky and tall as the bouncer with Janet Summerfield. Josh vaulted the front fence, and reached the door.

'Having a spot of bother?' he enquired over his shoulder, of Imogen.

'These people are just leaving,' she said.

'Oh, good. Well, we'll wait and see them off, shall we?' His heavyweight friend opened the gate, and bowed elaborately.

'You haven't heard the last of this!' said Janet Summerfield. 'We'll be back!' But she was beating a retreat now. A wide area of black coat topped by tousled grey hair was turned on Imogen. Her companion followed her, reluctantly. Obviously he had been longing for permission to shoulder the door and break the chain.

'Christ, Imogen,' said Simon, 'who's your fat friend? Was that the bailiffs? Good thing we were passing. This is Jason, and that's Wace. They like coffee and biscuits as much as I do.'

Imogen slipped the chain and let the boys in. 'You're all very welcome,' she said, 'but you'll have to fend for yourselves. I must get back to bed . . .' She was swaying gently on her feet.

'Put the kettle on, Jason,' said Josh, and he picked up Imogen bodily, and carried her upstairs, putting her down gently on the edge of her bed. 'A hot-water bottle and some Lemsip for you, I should think,' he said. 'We'll leave the door on the chain, and let ourselves out at the back when we go. But I think we'll lurk for a few minutes in case your heavies see us leaving and think to return. What have you been up to?'

'It isn't me,' Imogen told him, pulling the blankets up to her chin, and gasping with relief at the comforting warmth. 'It's Fran.'

'Curiouser and curiouser,' he said. 'Look, I'm sharing a room with Simon, and we're only in Chedworth Street. I'll write the telephone number in your phone book, in case you need to rabbit me out of a hat any time.'

'Thank you Josh. You're a pal. And you certainly came at the right moment just now.'

'What a hero I am,' said Josh smugly. 'Get some sleep, why don't you?'

For a while Imogen lay awake and aching. Josh appeared with a mug of Lemsip, and her hot-water bottle, and she tucked it under her toes. The sun had moved round the house far enough to flood her bedroom with morning light. Outside in the street she heard passing footfalls, and the occasional car. Downstairs the voices of her visitors and the chink of their mugs and spoons comforted her obscurely. Ever since childhood she had liked that feel a house has when someone in another room is talking, moving, humming – when there is a sense of life flowing within the walls. She did not hear them leave; she must have been asleep by then.

Imogen woke to find Fran in the room. She must just have come in – she was still wearing her jacket. 'Do you want some lunch?' she asked.

'Something to drink, perhaps,' said Imogen. Her throat felt dry. 'How did you get on with the Professor?'

'Badly,' said Fran. 'I'll bring you some soup and tell you about it.' Imogen struggled up to a sitting position in the bed, and waited. Fran reappeared with a mug of consommé, a glass of water and some aspirin.

'Anything else you want?' she enquired.

'Tell me how you got on,' said Imogen.

'He was angry with me. Very.'

'What for?'

'Pestering – his word – Janet Summerfield. I have overstepped my role, it seems. I was not supposed to conduct any enquiries, merely write up the material I was given. He had given his word that no embarrassing investigation would occur. I had a lot of trouble convincing him that I had not gone and told her he was not intending to write it himself. But of course, I had twigged that she didn't know that, and I hadn't told her. Only . . .'

'You had told her enough to let her know where to come for her papers, Fran,' said Imogen.

'What do you mean, come? Was she here?'

Imogen told Fran of the morning's brouhaha, but played down somewhat the general nastiness of the episode.

'What am I going to do?' asked Fran, dejectedly. 'This is going to be terrible if Professor Maverack won't support me. And *why* won't he? His whole theory of biography is that people are shit-holes, concealing their faults, deceiving themselves, presenting a false face to the world, and the biographer is to reveal the lies by which men live.'

'Perhaps he thinks one missing holiday doesn't amount to an interesting lie.'

'What about three missing biographers, then?' said Fran. 'Why has that happened if it isn't important? You know, at first, Imogen, I felt suspicious that he was going to edge my name off the title page, and take all the credit for the book himself without acknowledging me; now I wonder if it isn't the other way round . . .'

'What do you mean, Fran? I'm not at my brightest . . .'

'I'm sorry; it isn't fair to burden you with this when you're not well. I meant that now I wonder if the plan might be to lumber me with all the responsibility for the book – and make sure his own name is nowhere to be seen. That might explain why he wants to whitewash the subject.'

'That American said Maverack was a good example of his own theories . . .' mused Imogen. 'Look, this won't do. I think you might have to give back the family papers. After all, they are hers. But it's probably worth while to make sure nothing by the earlier workers goes back to her – I don't see how Mark Zephyr's files, or May Swann's notebooks can be hers, do you? Make sure everything is in separate piles, why don't you?'

'But can they come back and try again?'

'I don't know what they can do,' said Imogen. 'I've never met this sort of thing before.' She sounded, as she felt, sleepy. She must have drowsed before Fran left the room, she was not aware of her going.

By the following morning Imogen felt better – better enough to have a bath and get dressed, and go downstairs for a while. The aches and shakes had worn off and left her feeling languid and aimless. She ate as much breakfast as she could, and she was still sitting at the table, with the crossword propped on the marmalade jar, and completely blank, when a sharp crisp knock on the door interrupted her.

She opened the door to Janet Summerfield, this time accompanied by a man in a dark suit, and a policeman. 'My client obtained an *ex parte* hearing before a judge in chambers last night,' said the suited man. 'The judge has given us a Mareva injunction, to be served on one Frances Bullion, resident at this address. Is Frances Bullion at home, please?'

Behind Imogen Fran had come down the stairs, and now said, 'Yes I am.'

'I must deliver this document into your hands,' said the suit.

'Very well,' said Fran. She joined Imogen at the door, but Imogen reached out, and taking Fran's wrist prevented her from accepting the long narrow envelope.

'What is a Mareva injunction?' she asked.

'It is a writ. It prevents Frances Bullion and or her agents from destroying, defacing, concealing, or removing to any other premises the papers in dispute, until such time as an *intra partes* hearing can determine the suit between Janet Summerfield and the said Frances Bullion. It ensures the return of the papers intact and entire to Janet Summerfield, unless the said Frances Bullion can show cause before a properly constituted court why the papers should not be returned . . .'

'There is no need for this,' said Frances. 'I have not refused to return the documents. But . . . Mrs Summerfield—' Fran raised her voice slightly, addressing Janet Summerfield over the shoulder of the lawyer. 'If you remove the materials for the biography from me before I have completed the work, I cannot be responsible for the accuracy of the eventual book.'

'You will indeed not be responsible,' said Janet Summerfield. 'Another biographer will be found.'

'I am serving you with this writ, Miss Bullion,' said the lawyer. 'You must take it, please.'

Fran took the envelope from him, and at once the three in the deputation turned as if to leave. 'Well, do you want these papers, or don't you?' said Fran. 'Aren't you going to wait for them?' She put the envelope into Imogen's hand, and ran off up the stairs.

'Why did someone give you an order like that, when you were not faced with any refusal to return the papers?' said Imogen. She was shaking, not from flu, but with anger.

'On my client's sworn affidavit that a request for the return of the documents had been made, and refused, and further sworn undertaking to pay all necessary damages if the case stated turned out to be unfounded when the matter came before the jurisdiction of the court in the presence of the other party . . .'

'She is mad!' said Imogen. 'She was refused only because Miss Bullion was not at home when she called . . .'

Fran put a cardboard box of papers on the doorstep.

'Is this all?' asked the lawyer.

'No; there is a second box,' said Fran. 'I'll just get it.'

'We need a receipt for these items,' said Imogen, suddenly thinking of it.

'How do we know everything is there?' said Janet Summerfield. 'She could have kept things back.'

'These boxes,' said Fran, putting the second one beside the first, 'contain three hundred and six documents, of which most are of one page, and some forty are of two or more pages. Every original document which was given to me on behalf of Dr Maverack from the offices of Recktype and Diss is here.'

'But we will not hand them over without a written receipt,' said Imogen.

'I'm not giving you a receipt for my own property!' said Janet Summerfield.

'The request for a receipt is in good order, and should be complied with,' said the court bailiff suddenly. 'You may give a receipt for two boxes, contents unexamined, stated to contain three hundred and six items.'

'I . . .' began Janet Summerfield.

'You had better comply,' said the lawyer stonily. 'We will be in difficulty before the court if the facts are not as stated in your affidavit. If you comport yourself further in any way unreasonably you will not be a credible witness . . .' As he spoke he was writing in his notebook. He tore the page, and offered it to Janet Summerfield to sign.

And then the scene was over. The receipt was in Fran's hands, and the boxes were picked up from the doorstep and carried to the Mercedes parked across the street.

Imogen closed the door behind them. 'It's too late, anyway,' said Fran. 'I've read it all and made copies of the useful bits. And so help me God, Imogen, I'm going to give a proper account of Gideon Summerfield, whatever anyone says – the sanctified widow, the glorified professor, or the entire personnel of Recktype and Diss!'

'Or me,' said Imogen.

'Or you,' said Fran with an emphasis of finality.

10

The aftermath of flu is very depressive. Imogen didn't feel like staying out of bed, and she didn't feel like going back there. Fran had disappeared upstairs. The post brought three junk circulars, and a summons – a request on university crested letter paper for her appearance before the Court of Discipline in ten days' time. She looked at it blankly. She had no anger to spare for it. The undergraduate had an awful cheek, trying to blame Imogen for what he had been up to, but she was suffering, as a result of Janet Summerfield's interventions, from indignation fatigue.

On a sudden impulse she put her coat on and went out. It was such a beautiful day. She walked to the end of the road, intending to take the footpath to Grantchester, not all the way, on her first day out of bed, just a little distance. But she had got only as far as the paddock, where a few lucky youngsters kept ponies, before the point where the path opened out to the view of the serpentine, willow-lined river, when she felt she had gone far enough. Turning back she saw Shirl and Pansy approaching from the other end of the road, bearing stuffed pillowcases full of scraps. She waved, and they waited for her. She had forgotten they were coming.

'You look awful, Imogen,' said Pansy brightly. 'Should you be out?'

'No, not really,' said Imogen, 'but I'm in now. Come in and we'll get started.'

'Are you well enough?' asked Shirl. 'What is it? Flu?'

'After-effects of. Don't think I'm infectious.'

'We did rather want your advice. We've got twelve blocks to arrange, and the borders to design.'

'Giving advice never killed anyone,' said Imogen, smiling. 'The table in the sitting-room is clear. Spread it out.'

But the table was not big enough. When Fran came down half an hour later the three women were crawling round the floor, with the patchwork blocks laid out on the sitting-room carpet.

'Golly,' said Fran. 'What's afoot? I like those starry squares!'

'They look like compass stars when you see them one by one,' Pansy told her. 'But look what happens when you put them together.' She moved a group of squares closer on the carpet, so that the unhemmed edges overlapped slightly, and no border of carpet was visible between them. The background fabric, which appeared broken up as small areas round the edges of the block, narrow triangles between the spokes of the patterned stars, joined up when they were laid together, making plain stars between the patterned ones. You could see the quilt as made of multicoloured compass roses on a plain background, or as scattered with plain stars in an elaborate interwoven lattice of colour. There was a visual 'click' as you saw it first one way and then the other.

'Wow!' sad Fran. 'What a beautiful thing! I had no idea . . .'

'Good, isn't it?' said Shirl smugly.

'*Seriously* good,' said Fran. 'My Gran made patchwork quilts, and I thought they were all like hers. She used very tiny pieces all the same shape and just random colours and patterns all over. I never knew you could get an effect like that. No wonder Imogen is so keen.'

'This one is for a raffle for the Red Cross,' said Pansy. 'Feel like helping?'

'You bet. What needs doing?'

'We have to dream up a border,' said Pansy, 'choose the fabrics for it, work out the amounts needed, make cardboard templates, and mark and cut the shapes. Then we have to put the right amounts of each shape and colour for about a foot of border into each of these plastic bags to take to our jolly team of needle-persons to sew.'

'Is that all?' said Fran laughing. 'Give me some unskilled work. I approve of your gender awareness, by the way.'

'How about ironing swatches for us, so that they are flat enough to cut accurately?' suggested Imogen.

'Anyone who helps gets to help choose colours,' said Shirl. 'And it isn't so much that Pansy is gender-aware, I'm sorry to say, it's simply that one of the needlewomen in the Quilters' Club is factually a man. Actually Pansy is a rather unreconstructed, pre-modernist sort of woman.'

'I sew a straighter seam than you do, for all that,' said Pansy equably.

'Do all possible designs have a repeat like that one?' asked Fran, contemplating the arrangement on the floor from her viewpoint at the ironing board.

'There are lots of different effects,' said Shirl. 'But every pattern repeats. Your gran's type of work repeated with every single shape – this repeats with every block. You could have a repeat of every second or third block . . .'

By and by Fran graduated from ironing to marking and cutting shapes. The women worked steadily and pleasantly together, and chatted. Remembering that Shirl worked part-time in a firm of solicitors in Petty Curie, Imogen thought to ask her if she knew what a Mareva injunction was.

'A freeze. Stops everything exactly as it is while some dispute gets sorted out.'

'Why Mareva?'

'It's the name of a ship. There was a dispute over harbour dues or somesuch, and the ship was about to sail out of British jurisdiction. The injunction held it at its moorings while the courts heard the dispute. I don't know much about it, I'm afraid. I could look it up, or ask Bob.'

'No need,' said Imogen. 'I just wondered. The crisis is past.'

Which led, of course, to Imogen and Fran telling the dramatic story of the recovery of the papers, and the job Fran was doing for Dr Maverack. Fran avoided, Imogen noticed, mentioning the earlier biographers, but she explained the missing August. And Pansy suddenly dropped a bombshell.

'If I wanted to know something about old Gideon, I'd ask Melanie,' she said.

'Who's Melanie?' asked Fran.

'Melanie Bratch. She was his mistress for years and years. She might know.'

Fran stood thunderstruck, holding a pair of scissors poised to cut and motionless, while she stared at Pansy. 'He had a mistress?' she asked.

'More than one, the horrid old goat. But Melanie was mistress in chief.'

'But . . . there isn't a sign of it, not a murmur in any of the papers we told you about.'

'A successfully kept secret?' asked Imogen.

'Hardly that. He used to have tea with her once a week, and if he couldn't make it, Janet would ring up and change the day or time for him. Used to give me the creeps to think about it, but Melanie didn't seem to mind. And she went with them in the summer more than once when they rented a villa in Tuscany. Smelly or civilised according to your point of view.'

'Pansy, however do you know all this?' asked Imogen.

'Melanie is my best friend. Well, one of them.'

Fran turned to Imogen, her brow furrowed, her eyes wide. 'Janet Summerfield must have kept back stuff. She must have removed evidence of a mistress . . .'

'So why all the heat about getting papers back, if she censored what she lent?'

'A mistake. She made a mistake. There was *something* in those papers that she realised too late would give the game away about the mistresses . . .' Fran stopped, puzzled. 'But I can't think what it was. There wasn't anything . . . I hadn't a clue.'

'Pansy, are you absolutely sure?' asked Shirl.

'Absolutely. Melanie was crazy about him.'

'She couldn't have been fantasising?'

'Over ten years? Why would she? It would have been a very prolonged and elaborated fib. Anyway the point I'm making is, why not ask her?'

'Wild horses wouldn't stop me,' said Fran. 'Where is she?'

'Just up the Histon Road. She lived in Buckden for years, but she's moved into sheltered housing – old people's flats. I've got the address.'

Pansy reached into her handbag for her address book, and in her eagerness to take the precious information down Fran put down the iron on a swatch of cloth, and scorched it while she wrote.

Shirl scolded, serenely, and cut the scorched area out of the piece. 'Remind me not to ask for your help making shirts or curtains,' she said.

'I don't know what kind of light it casts on human nature,' Fran said to Imogen later, as they cleared up the threads and clippings from almost every surface in the sitting-room, after Shirl and Pansy had departed, 'but it's the only interesting thing yet to emerge about the great Gideon.'

I I

It was, on account of the flu, some few days since Imogen had been in college, and a large bundle of files for new undergraduates awaited her. She worked hard all morning on filing, and scanning, reading rapidly over the forms new students filled in, looking for anything medical of which she had better be aware. At twelve she felt jaded. 'Serves you right, Imogen,' she told herself. How often had she scolded a flu victim for getting back to work too quickly? But served right or not, she felt like a sherry before lunch, and on impulse decided to exercise her privilege, conferred on her by a grateful college, and go and have a drink in the senior common room.

It was a handsome room, in the Victorian wing of the college, looking out on to the stretch of the garden that contained the Castle Mound. The tall windows were in full sun, and motes of dust hovered like minute insects in the slanting beams of warm light. The room had the anonymous comfort of a good club. On a side-table were arrayed pretty well all the national papers, as well as yesterday's *Cambridge Evening News*. Lord knows against whose names the original requests for the *Sun* and the *Star* had been entered, but the universally approved result was that everyone could read, or at least glance at, the pop papers, and nobody had to buy them. The college fellows could display very well-informed disdain for the gutter press.

Imogen helped herself to sherry from the range of decanters on a handsome sideboard, selected *New Scientist* which was offering an article on pollen dating by a college fellow, and settled in one of the vast pneumatically soft armchairs. At once someone who had been sitting comfortably at the far end of the room rose, and moved towards her. Professor Maverack. She lowered her eyes to the printed page, and feigned to be lost in reading, but undeterred he sat down opposite, and said, 'May I join you?'

Imogen nodded. One cannot, after all, say 'no'.

'I am told,' he said, after a decent interval, 'that Frances Bullion is your lodger.'

'Yes,' said Imogen.

'Rather more, I gather – she is a close friend?'

'I am pleased to think so,' said Imogen coldly, levelling her steadiest gaze at him.

'Forgive me. I don't mean to be impertinent. I have been asking around to find, if I can, someone who might have some influence with her, and Dr Bent suggested you.'

'You are her supervisor, aren't you?' said Imogen. 'Don't you have any influence over her?'

'Not enough,' he said. 'I'm sorry, I'm not going about this very well; but I do need to talk to someone about Miss Bullion. I realise that it's a delicate matter, but . . .'

Overcome with curiosity, Imogen tried to thaw her voice a bit. 'I can always be talked to,' she said. 'It's a large part of my job.'

'Thank you,' he said. 'You see, I'm afraid I may inadvertently have got Miss Bullion into trouble. And yet . . . I may be fanciful. I hope I am, but . . .' He halted, looking miserable.

'Dr Maverack,' said Imogen sternly, 'I hope you are not going to tell me that you gave Frances the Summerfield biography, knowing that it was likely to lead her into personal danger. Because if you did that, how can you expect any friend of hers to listen to anything you say?'

Oddly, he seemed relieved. 'I have less explaining to do than I thought,' he said. He looked round, making sure that no armchair in easy earshot was occupied. 'Please believe me, I had no intention whatever of leading her into danger. I simply thought the money would be of use to her. Of course I knew the project had been in difficulties; I had no idea *what* difficulties. Indeed, I can still hardly believe . . . I am probably just imagining things . . .' He seemed to collect himself. 'Frances has surprised me in two ways. Firstly, in discovering the existence of more than one former biographer; I knew of one, but only yesterday when she visited me did I know there had been three – *three*! Secondly, I had supposed that a research student would be, shall we say, biddable. That if I told her to ignore the remaining unanswered questions – if I told her that there always were loose ends and lost knowledge in any biography, she would simply accept it, and leave sleeping dogs alone. Whereas in fact, she announced her intention to defy me, and to pursue the truth, as she calls it, come hell or high water.'

'I take it you want me to try to dissuade Fran from further

investigation? But I might say that I thought such a devotion to the truth was a sign of a good scholar, and that you ought to be delighted rather than discouraging.'

'I don't suppose you are a statistician,' he said. 'But what would you say the chances were of three people coming to a sticky end, or vanishing off the face of the earth or something, in succession, and all of them working on the same thing, and the accidents being just pure chance, pure coincidence, nothing to do with the work in hand?'

'It is a bit strange, isn't it?' she conceded. 'The only one I have any knowledge of is Mark Zephyr, and he died of meningitis, and I honestly don't see how that could possibly be connected with working on a biography.'

'Well, I don't know anything about any of this string of mishaps,' he said. 'But the thing is, if they are coincident accidents, then the odds are long – longer with each successive person. And if they aren't coincidences, then they aren't accidents. Or so it seems to me.'

'And if they aren't accidents?'

'Then it would seem to be very dangerous to work on the Summerfield book. And Miss Bullion . . . and you see, I feel very badly about it. It is my fault she is – might be in a position of danger.'

'Dr Maverack,' said Imogen, 'can you tell me exactly why you off-loaded this commission on a student instead of doing it yourself?'

'It looks a bit bad, you mean? Yes, I see that it does. And it's ironic, really. I thought it would be boring. What interests me professionally is the discovery of deceit. The demolition of the pathetic false idealisations of self by which people live . . . I thought old Summerfield was not capable of being interestingly demolished. Too unimaginative to have erected for himself a grand false façade. I checked up with some mathematicians, and found that the maths is thought to be genuine – a real discovery, though an appendage to Penrose, it seems. Penrose discovered these funny patterns which don't repeat to infinity in any direction, but if you rotate them have some kind of ghostly five-sided quality. He set the mathematical world by the ears with them. They are huge fun, I am told. Summerfield came up with a variant kind, ghostly heptagons. Also fun.'

'Not easily demolished?'

'Not by a non-mathematician, for sure.'

A thoughtful silence fell between them. Then, 'Dr Maverack . . .'

'Do call me Leo. I hardly recognise myself otherwise.'

'A doctorate by way of false façade?' said Imogen, amused in spite of herself. He had the grace to blush slightly. 'Leo – should we tell the police?'

'I've tried that. They let me make a long and involved statement to a very young policeman, who wrote it down in full. They said they would report my statement to officers in charge of the relevant investigations. But they clearly regarded me as mad. They were very concerned to know what I took the motive to be for suppressing biographers. And of course, I didn't know.'

'Naturally I have wondered about that too. Janet Summerfield certainly seems fierce enough . . .'

'But it is she who wants the biography; cares passionately that it should be out in time for the Waymark Prize . . .' he said.

'But if there is a dark secret, she would want it kept dark?'

'What dark secret?'

'His mistress, perhaps?' offered Imogen.

'Oh, that. But everybody who knew him knows about that. You couldn't possibly expect to keep it secret.'

'Fran said there was absolutely nothing about it in the papers she was given. She found out by sheer accident.'

'Really? How very odd. Melanie isn't a disgrace of any kind, anyway, not nowadays. Rather a feather in the old bore's cap, I would have thought. She was a very beautiful woman.'

'You knew her?'

'I knew them all, long ago. When we were all young. Before I went to America. But, look, Imogen. Whatever is behind all this the obviously best thing is for Frances to get an anodyne book written as fast as possible, and for her to stop, absolutely stop ferreting around for more material, and then she'll be out of harm's way, and we can all relax. However, she reacted very forcibly and volubly to this suggestion coming from me. Really, I am hoping you can make her see sense.'

'I could try. But not with much hope of succeeding. She is very much her own woman.'

'Don't I know it!' he said, ruefully. 'I'm all for equality; truly I am. But it does make the fair sex combative!'

Imogen stood up. The tactfully muted bell had signalled lunch, and she intended to eat in hall today. Very much in spite of herself she was rather liking Leo Maverack. 'There's something else I can.

and will do,' she told him. 'I have a friend in the police here. I'll try to find out if they have really put your statement in the bin, or if there is anything happening.'

'That's a good idea,' he said, hauling himself out of the deep cushions of his chair. 'That would be good to know. But the main thing, you know, is to safeguard Frances, in case . . .'

'There is mischief rather than accident at work?'

'Precisely.'

'I'll try,' she told him.

Later, as Imogen was leaving college, she saw, as she strolled through the gateway arch, pinned on a board that was covered three deep with handbills, posters and announcements, an announcement for a special lecture in the Mill Lane lecture room – Dr Holly Portland on the dating of eighteenth- and nineteenth-century printed silk and cotton textiles. Imogen stopped and noted the date and time in her diary. She would go to that, and take Shirl and Pansy with her if they were free.

Imogen had expected Fran to be difficult to advise; somehow she had not expected a flaming row. Within a few minutes of the conversation beginning Fran had extracted the confession that Imogen had been talking to Professor Maverack. She froze, and regarded Imogen coldly across the room.

'And are we to expect in due course monographs on the contributions of landladies to twentieth-century biographical scholarship?' she enquired.

'Fran . . .'

'No, Imogen. This is not a minor medical emergency. Unless there is a swathe of your early life which you have never mentioned to me, the truth is you have no relevant expertise, and no standing. You are in no position to tell me whether I should or should not investigate something to do with my professional work.'

'Fran, calm down a minute . . .'

'You have the damn cheek to discuss me behind my back with my supervisor . . .'

'Fran . . .'

'I'd be bloody angry with you if you were my mother, Imogen, and you're not even a second cousin twice removed. Just mind your own bloody business, will you?'

And with that Fran flounced out, banging the door.

'Whew!' said Imogen, sitting down abruptly. When the shock wore off in a moment or two, misery would engulf her, she knew. But before it did the phone rang.

'I'm back.' It was Mike's voice. 'How about a spot of lunch, and a walk?'

'Oh, oh Mike. That sounds nice. Next Sunday?'

'Sooner. Today if you like.'

'Aren't you at work?'

'I've taken a few extra days leave to recover from the holiday. Are you all right, Imogen? Have I put my foot in it somehow? You don't sound your usual delighted-to-hear-from-you self.'

'Mike, of course I'm delighted. I'm just upset about something – nothing to do with you. And today would be wonderful . . .'

'You do rather sound as if you could do with some cheering from big brother Mike Parsons. If it's nothing to do with me, is it anything to do with disappeared persons?'

'Remotely. I'll tell you about it on this proposed walk.'

'Certainly, I could find out if anyone is working on Professor Maverack's report,' said Mike. 'But I'm pretty sure his impression will be right – they will have taken his statement to humour him, and put it on file, and got back to work.'

They were standing on the top of Linton Hill, just beyond the water tower, where the trees thinned out, and a splendid view spread out below them. Not that Linton Hill is *high*, exactly, – it must be a rise of less than a hundred feet, but in so flat a county it nevertheless gives a dizzying prospect. The mere fact that the land is softly folded, and you can see a long way on the blue level landscape below, and look down on the little town – or is it a big village? – is refreshingly heady. Last year there had been a blazing fluorescent yellow field of rape down there at the foot of the slope; this year there was a field of flax, grey-blue, and looking like a lake of standing water under a cloudy sky.

'But Mike, why? *Why* aren't the police interested?'

'Their job is solving crime, not solving conundrums.'

'But this might *be* crime; several crimes.'

'Well . . . What have we got here? A funny coincidence. And a worry on your part that something might happen to a friend of yours. A friend who is so far in bouncing good health.'

'But . . .'

'Bear with me. I'm answering your question. Now, if there had been a string of three crimes – something, we know not what, that befell Ian Goliard; a disappearance which indicates a crime against May Swann, and a death from apparently natural causes, which you are implying was not natural at all . . .'

'I never said that. Meningitis is . . .'

'You are implying that. You must be. If these crimes have taken place, the motivation of the criminal is unusual – bizarre. It isn't anything like the motives the police are used to. It isn't lust, jealousy, filthy lucre, revenge or rage. It isn't self-defence. It is some arcane matter to do with biography. The biography of a dead don who seems to have lived a boring and law-abiding life. Honestly, Imogen, what a farrago. And the police are busy.'

'I see. And if something were to happen to Frances, what then?'

'That would take a bit of laughing off, I agree.'

'So three dead bodies could be coincidence, but a fourth . . .'

'But we haven't *got* three dead bodies, woman! Your May Swann may turn up any minute – dead or alive. And who knows what happened to Ian Goliard? Perhaps he won the pools, and swanned off to Florida.'

'Could one find out?'

'Might be able to. Tell you what, I'll try. All right? Now, aren't you ever going to ask me about my holiday?'

12

'I'm sorry,' said Fran.

'No, I'm sorry,' said Imogen.

'But I didn't mean . . .' said both at once. They laughed.

'Of course I've no right to be worried about you,' said Imogen.

'Since when didn't a best friend have a right to be worried?' said Fran. 'I'm just on edge, I think. I'm so bloody determined not to be bullied and deflected and pushed into doing a job badly, that I'm firing off with all guns in every direction at friend and foe alike.'

'Good description,' said Imogen, ruefully. 'But the rebuke was in order.'

'Whether or no, let's make it up. I've got a lot to tell you,' said Fran.

It was a fine morning, and the two women went through the back door into the tiny garden. An old, solid wooden bench, weathered silver-grey, stood on a small area of York paving slabs, under the kitchen window, facing south. A china rose scrambled up the fence beside it sporting a few brave, late blossoms. Beyond the tiny lawn an ancient gnarled apple tree filled the garden from fence to fence, covered with hard little green apples and dappled golden light. They sat, closing their eyes and tilting their heads to the bright October morning.

'I saw Melanie,' said Fran.

'And?' said Imogen, opening her eyes, and sitting up.

'I learned a lot,' said Fran. 'She talked and talked. I had trouble getting away.'

'Tell, tell.'

'Well, I have to précis. She knew Summerfield all their lives, pretty much. Before they were students together. They met at a tennis club in Palmer's Green. She was mildly sweet on him, but she had a lot of other boyfriends. Then when he went up to Cambridge, Janet made a dead set at him, and Melanie played it cool, and lost him. She kept right on seeing him – them – though. There was a tight

little group of friends, who kept up with each other. Odd thing –
Professor Maverack seems to have been one of them, until he took
a job in the States. Did you realise *that?*'

'He told me,' said Imogen.

'You didn't say . . .'

'You bit my head off before I had a chance. Go on.'

'And – get this! – Another of the group was one Ian Goliard.'

'Ho, ho. The plot thickens . . .'

'You bet. Now Melanie knows a good deal about Ian Goliard.'

'As, like, where he is?'

'No, she doesn't know that. But she knows he took on the biography in the first place as a tribute to an old friend. He's very rich, I
gather: it wasn't for the money, it was to be an elegant memoir of the
great man. But he quickly went off the idea. According to Melanie he
was being hounded by Janet, who was loading him down with family
papers and old diaries and such, enough to fill an entire encylopaedia,
whereas what he had in mind was a slender volume, devoted mainly
to a great scholar's contribution to the world of learning . . . and
whereas on the one hand she was demanding that he devoted months
to reading Giddy's laundry lists . . .'

'*Whose?*'

Fran laughed. 'Isn't it odd? I've got so used to thinking of him
as a monster patriarch, and she calls him "old Giddy"! You know,
Imogen, she has such an affectionate, amused tone when she talks
about him, she made him come real to me. Somebody really *liked*
him – you know that? Where was I?'

'Goliard. On the one hand forced to read laundry lists . . .'

'And on the other hand she became venomously hostile when he
proposed to retrace old Giddy's steps, and visit some places in the
life. Melanie says Goliard was a poet; published in small presses,
and he rather wanted to spread himself on background landscapes
– places where the great man had trod – that sort of book. When it
became clear Janet would obstruct him, he took himself abroad. Just
dumped the project back to the publishers. Melanie knows he did; he
left her to post the papers back, under plain cover.'

'And where did he go?'

'Thailand, probably. Or perhaps China. He's rich; and he has
boyfriends all over the place. He can lie low in comfort for as
long as he likes. His friends have never had addresses for him. One
writes care of a bank in London.'

'Well, that seems to complete the strange prehistory of the biography. All the hands in the papers accounted for.'

'Yes. And it seems clearer than ever to me that there is something Janet Summerfield doesn't want known . . .'

'And that that something has to do with a place, somewhere . . .'

'Where he spent the missing summer of '78. Looks like it, doesn't it?'

'Well, did you ask Melanie about it? What did she say?'

'She was hugely helpful, but it doesn't help.'

'Explain.'

'Well, it seems that usually they all went on holiday together.'

'All?'

'Janet and "Giddy" and Melanie – they called her Melon, and Ian and several other friends from Cambridge days. Someone called Meredith, even, once, Maverack. They would rent a Chalet in the Alps, or a cottage on Exmoor or the Lakes, and all descend on it with cases of wine, and hampers from Fortnums, and the Scrabble board – she says he was a demon at Scrabble – and they would tumble about, getting into each other's beds, and sleeping late, and walking every afternoon. Old Giddy used to call this their summer Saturnalias.'

Something in Fran's tone made Imogen ask, 'How does that strike you, Fran? As a way to carry on, I mean.'

'Yucky. Pathetic.'

'I expect it seemed immensely liberated to them, at the time.'

'Oh, yes, so I gathered. It gave Melanie her chance. But I wouldn't have taken it, in her place. It must have been hellish painful, especially when the holiday was over and they all came home, Janet and Gideon to married bliss in Bottisham and Melanie to a lonely flat.'

'Wherein she was visited weekly . . .'

'He was sent.'

'What?'

'Janet sent him. She reckoned that if the old goat had deflowered the virgin Melanie, it was up to him to keep her serviced until she found an alternative source of satisfaction. She didn't, so it went on for years. Till he died, in fact.'

'My father used to say "nowt so queer as folk",' Imogen remarked.

'Spot on,' said Fran. 'And queerer than you yet know, Imogen. Because pretty soon Melanie and Old Giddy didn't normally fancy sex together. Just because it had happened once or twice

under the influence of wine and Tuscan sun, during one of
the Saturnalias, didn't mean that they really wanted a steamy
affair continuing indefinitely.'

'Well, but what made them . . .'

'He didn't fancy confessing to Janet that he wasn't required;
Melanie didn't fancy confessing to her arch rival that she didn't
have any pull; they were fond of each other. So sometimes it was
a cover for another assignation, and sometimes they just had a cup
of tea and a quiet chat. They intended originally, I gather, to tell
Janet some time; then they got used to their weekly tête-à-tête . . .
anyway they never did tell her.'

'And can you put all or any of that into the biography, for all,
including Janet, to read?'

'If I like. Melanie doesn't seem to mind. While Summerfield was
alive she wouldn't have liked to precipitate a row with Janet, but
now she seems very laid back about it all.'

'How *very* odd, though,' said Imogen thoughtfully, 'that one might
need to keep it secret that one was *not* sleeping with someone . . .'

'Well, they're all more or less bats,' said Fran cheerfully. 'But I sort
of understand. Don't you think – if he visited Melanie constantly for
all those years, and it wasn't sex, then it would have to be love – true
affection. And it might be much easier for a lawfully wedded wife to
think of her dear one as oversexed and needing auxiliary supplies,
than to think of sharing his true affection . . . *I* think . . .'

'I expect you're right,' said Imogen. 'It sounds very romantic, but
it still might be true. How clever of you to work it out . . . But do I
gather Melanie doesn't know about the missing August? She sounds
as though she would know just about everything.'

'Yes; but not that. She remembers August '78 very clearly. They
rented a cottage at Colwall, in the Malverns. They were going to climb
the hills and look down at fair fields full of folk. But what actually
happened was a terrible row. The cottage was too small; someone
had brought a friend, and it was crowded. Someone accused Gideon
of cheating at Scrabble. Hard words were spoken, and Gideon left.'

'With or without Janet?'

'Without Janet, but with Meredith's friend. Melanie hasn't a clue
where they went. They came back four days later, not speaking to
each other. It cast a dampener on the summer's entertainment for
everyone.'

'I should think it did!'

'But Melanie honestly truly doesn't know where Gideon went. She was very cross with him about it at the time, and so she never mentioned the episode to him afterwards. The next year Meredith turned up without friend . . .'

'No wonder . . . but Frances, where do you go from here?'

'Don't know, quite. I'll mull it over.'

'You won't be satisfied with all that new material, and simply record the story as you've just told me, and be damned to those four days?'

'Nope,' said Fran, stretching, and getting up. She wandered across and put her nose into a big blowsy rose, which responded by shedding its petals lavishly at her feet.

'I think I've got further than any of others. It would be real cowardy custard to give up now. Incidentally, what's so cowardly about custard? Do you know?'

'Haven't a clue. I've known some custard in my time that would require a tad of courage . . .'

'Haven't we all?' said Fran, darkly.

13

Holly's lecture on the dating of fabric was at five in the Mill Lane Lecture Rooms. It was a cold and blustery evening, with bursts of rain on the gusts of wind, and a wintry feel to the world. When Shirley and Pansy arrived to pick up Imogen the three friends decided to drive, and park in the Lion Yard, if there wasn't any room in Silver Street. A sullenly dramatic light overhung the city; wet streets, gleaming, a cloudscape above full of lowering blackness and silver cloud rims; people scuttling under rain-glossed umbrellas; the buildings looming in the daylight dimness – the few shops on their route showing golden rectangles of warm lighting, and casting angled rectangles of light across the pavements.

The lecture room was very thinly packed; not more than thirty people at most, but the weather gave a painless alibi for that. Imogen sat between Shirley and Pansy, and all three of them had brought notebooks and pencils, in the expectation of enlightenment. Holly was sitting at the table at the front, putting slides into a carousel, while a technician set up the projector. She looked up and waved at someone, and looking round Imogen saw Professor Maverack, making his way to the front. The lecture room had filled up considerably in the last few minutes. Professor Maverack stood out somewhat, since the audience was predominantly of women, and Imogen was briefly surprised to see him, until she remembered that Holly had talked of him as a friend. Presumably it was the lecturer rather than the subject that had brought him. At the very last minute a group of dignitaries filed in; governors of the Fitzwilliam, committee members of the friends of the Fitzwilliam, and Holly stood up to the microphone, and began.

Imogen learned an enormous amount in the next hour. How wildly desirable to Europeans Indian printed calicos had been, right through the eighteenth century – soft, wearable, washable with their lovely printed patterns in fast dyes. How the Indians had mastered the skills of mordant dying long before western manufacturers. How frantic attempts to proscribe the wearing of calicos, and impose

95

huge tariffs on them in protection of the wool and silk weavers at home had failed miserably. All that had been achieved was making people hoard every scrap and cutting of the precious calico, to reuse in quilts. Holly's slides traced the progress of printed designs – the East India Company's men in London sending requests for patterns in the English taste: 'Those which hereafter you shall send we desire may be with more white ground, and the flowers and branches to be in colours in the middle of the quilt as the painter pleases, whereas now the most part of your quilts come with sad red grounds which are not equally sorted to please all buyers . . .'

The English needlewomen were soon imitating Indian patterns in their needlework, and the Indian print makers imitating English needlework in their printed cottons, until it was impossible to disentangle the taste of the makers from the taste of the wearers of the fabrics. The history of fashion could be dimly traced in the inventory of cotton goods seized by the excise men from smugglers . . . Imogen watched entranced while Holly showed slides of old fabrics. Her last set of slides however was most interesting of all. She was discoursing on a new industry in America, of faking old quilts. Old quilts had become highly collectable, and so naturally people were trying to turn a dishonest buck by making new ones look old. Holly showed a faded and worn quilt of great charm. Then she showed close-ups of the wear and fading on one of its pieces, alongside a faded piece of a truly old bedcover. You could see the difference at once. On the fake the wear and tear was random – or rather – look closely, Holly exhorted them – it was concentrated in places where it could be seen. On the really old pieces the wear was concentrated at the edge of the patches, where they pulled on each other, and over ridges where the seams overlapped, and the cloth was at its thickest, and over lumps in the carded but unspun wool with which the quilt was filled. In the fake piece the fading turned into the seams; in the old piece the material in the seams when you unpicked them was still bright. But in any case, Holly said, and Imogen could see what she meant, anyone with any kind of eye for it could see at once from some indefinable atmosphere in the patterns on the scraps whether they were old or not. She finished with a long sequence of slides of quilts, each one dated, and ranged in order from the bedhangings of Levens Hall, the oldest surviving patchwork, datable to 1708, right through to quilts made in the fifties. Like those timed sequences which show you flowers opening on the stalk, the sequence showed the changing shapes and colours of fashion. Once Holly's historical prospectus reached Imogen's own lifetime she found it amazingly recognisable -- the quilts might have been made from her own clothes and those of her friends. She still winced at the sulphur yellows and bright turquoise patterns of the fifties! And though the fabrics changed, the blocks and their repeating structure remained, done in a thousand hues, a kaleidoscopic mosaic of prints, but themselves strongly traditional, handed down the generations of women, their folksy names and persistent appearance and reappearance telling of mother and daughter, and church sewing circle, reaching way back.

After the lecture Holly was surrounded by admirers, Leo Maverack among them, and Imogen slipped away, and had a drink in the Anchor with her two friends before going home. She went to bed with a book, and instead of reading, let her mind wander over the many quilts Holly had shown. Some of them, of course, had been made by prosperous housewives, with time and money to spare, because they preferred their own handiwork to what could be bought. But many – most – were made by poor and ordinary women from practical need. And who were all these people, with a nimble needle, and an eye for colour and pattern? The least of them achieved a charm and prettiness found in very few designed and manufactured things; the best of them had made visually stunning pieces, that would steal the show if hung on the walls of art galleries instead of spread on beds, and washed and worn to bits. Imogen had recently read a whole book on the question why all the great painters were men. It offered a number of reasons, of varying degrees of plausibility, but had not suggested that the reason was that the women worked in textiles instead of oil or watercolour.

Imogen felt an enormous and heart-warming solidarity with all these women of the past – mute inglorious Elizabeths and Janes, whose work didn't count as art. She began to dream up her own masterpiece, based on one of the blocks she had just seen.

There was a light tap on the door, and Fran's voice, very quiet. 'Imogen? Are you awake?'

'Come!' called Imogen. Fran came in, and sat in the little nursing chair, over which Imogen cast her clothes at night, unceremoniously dumping the clothes on the floor.

'I thought you must be awake,' she said, 'since the light was on.'

'I'm just thinking,' said Imogen.

'Funny coincidence; I've been thinking too.'

'What about?'

'About biographers, actually. Being one, that is. Suppose, for a fr'instance, one had a subject who had one glorious year . . .'

'Like Keats?'

'. . . and one spent ten years researching him and writing about him. It's quite a thought, isn't it - the proportion of one's own life engrossed in someone else's? You could in theory spend all the years of your own life elucidating someone else's, and that couldn't be sensible unless the subject was immensely more important and interesting than oneself. Well, no doubt the subjects of biography ought to be that - worth their own years and a stretch of someone else's to the world - but when you look actually you find that lots of published biographies are about folk of quite modest importance - people dimly heard of but nearly forgotten, or some famous person's wife, or . . .'

'In my experience people's wives are often more interesting than they are,' said Imogen drily.

'Well, the remark wasn't intended to be gender-specific; a famous person's husband would be an equally clear example.'

'I rather think my remark wasn't gender-specific either; I meant that given a couple, the less famous one is often . . .'

'I hadn't noticed that; but I expect you're right.'

'The real question is, why do people spend long years celebrating minor stars in the constellation?'

'To earn a living?'

'To enable themselves to be professional writers?'

'To make some worthwhile contribution to the state of knowledge?'

'To defeat oblivion?'

'Both for the subject and for themselves . . .'

'Well, your biography appears to be a short cut *to* oblivion for the biographer . . .'

'I'm being careful - honest.'

'The sooner you get round to researching autobiography the better I'll like it.'

'I never know quite what I do to earn your affection, Imogen,' said Fran, 'but what I really came to ask is, do you want a few days in Wales?'

'With you? Sounds good. When?'

'Leave tomorrow, or the day after?'

Imogen reached for her diary, and saw the snag at once. 'I've got to be in Cambridge the day after tomorrow, Fran,' she said. 'Could it wait till next week?'

'Blast!' said Fran. 'Oh, well, I'll have to go by myself. Unless you could change your appointment?'

But it was the Court of Discipline. 'I would if I could, love,' said Imogen regretfully. 'But Wales won't run away . . .'

'Another time, then,' said Fran. 'Good night.'

The Court of Discipline was held in the Old Schools. Oddly, though Imogen had passed down Trinity Lane times without number, going through King's College on her way to and fro, or taking the spectacularly beautiful way through Clare College, she had never stepped through the somewhat forbidding arch into the looming Victorian Gothic building. But inside the courtyard one came face to face with a pretty, church-like medieval building, modestly completing a courtyard the Victorian improvers had tried hard to make grand. Imogen entered by a door in the south range, and found herself in an interior which the incumbent University Registry had tried hard to make office-like. She was directed upstairs.

The accused young man had, as was usual, requested that the hearing be held in camera, and that the two junior members of the University, who could have made up a panel with the two senior members, not be appointed. It was very rare for anyone to want two of his fellow students to adjudicate; even rarer for anyone to want the hearing to be held in public. When Imogen arrived, therefore, there were three men sitting behind the table – the chairman and two senior members – and the defendant was sitting stiff and white-faced beside his Senior Tutor. The lawyer he had threatened to use was not there after all.

The proctor entered a formal complaint on behalf of the University, and the University Advocate acting as prosecutor began to state the case to be answered.

The defendant had written a brilliant, even flawless answer paper. The question had involved some working out in logic – and the defendant's calculations were on a sheet of paper that had been folded, and then flattened out again. The sheet in question was the third of nine sheets he had used. It was the only one that had been folded. It carried the crucial material on which the high marks awarded to him had been based. In addition to having been folded, it had a little groove visible on all four quarters of the paper. The Advocate took up a clean sheet of paper, folded it, clipped his pen to the folded paper, removed the pen, flattened the paper and invited the panel to compare the sheet to the defendant's exam paper.

The two sheets of paper were passed round, and carefully examined; tipped this way and that in the light by each person in turn. Imogen sat quietly at the back, watching. In particular she watched Framingham. He was sitting very erect, and very tight-lipped. In front of him on the table was a notepad in which he occasionally scrawled something. The set of his head on his shoulders was odd, she thought – as though he had a stiff neck. His face was tilted a little upwards, and his glance was bent downwards to compensate. Defiance? Obstinacy? Misery, certainly – he positively radiated it. Well, it couldn't be fun, after all, to be accused of cheating.

The Court was carefully stepping through the situation. Luffincott's winning paper for the Random Prize; the startling resemblance between Framingham's final paper and Luffincott's prize essay; the folded exam paper . . . things were certainly looking rather bad for young Framingham.

The University Advocate began to put questions to him directly. 'Why was the sheet of paper folded?'

'I finished early. I was shuffling the papers, and messing about. I must have folded that one without thinking.'

'Precisely into four?'

'It's a nervous habit. Some people chew their pencils, I fold paper.' He extended his notebook to them. The page he had been writing on was folded in two.

Odd, Imogen thought. She had not seen him do it. The Advocate thought it was odd too.

'Your nerves impelled you to fold only one of nine sheets of paper, and that one the most important to the argument in your essay.'

'I did it without thinking. It's just chance it happened to be that one. I suppose it was on top.'

'And your nervous habit extends to clipping your pen to the edge of the folded sheet?'

'I told you. I was messing about.'

'Most people spend the time anxiously checking what they have written. You were not anxious?'

'No,' the boy said. 'Why should I be? I knew I had done well.'

'You knew that you had written precisely what had won the Random Prize for another man.'

'In a way. But not the way you are suggesting. I had discussed the matter with Luffincott, and with others in our group. We had worked out the best approach to the problem in conversation together. What's wrong with that? You don't accuse Luffincott of pinching his ideas from me!'

'It seems that Luffincott has been a high-flyer during the whole of his career at Cambridge, and if he has worked out an original approach to a crux in logic nobody is surprised; whereas your supervisor is very surprised to discover that you have done so.'

'I don't get on with him,' said Framingham. 'He doesn't like me.'

'Are you saying he has made a false report of your ability out of personal dislike?'

'Not exactly. But I didn't like him so I didn't work hard for him. I messed him about. He doesn't know what I can do.'

'So you are saying that in spite of your supervisor's view of your abilities, you did write this paper entirely yourself?'

'Yes.'

Both Framingham's college tutor, and his head of college, sitting either side of him, tried to draw his attention.

'. . . that is, yes, but under the influence of some medication. I remember feeling exceptionally alert and fast-reacting.'

'And you wish to call a witness, I believe?'

'Yes. Miss Quy.'

Imogen found herself called forward.

'You remember giving me pills?' Framingham asked her.

'I have a record of giving you something to help you sleep. You came to me late in the afternoon of 4th of June, and told me you were worried about the exams, and could not sleep. I gave you two paracetamol.'

'It can't have been paracetamol. It was a mind-bender. It put me on a high.'

'I have a record in my medication book,' Imogen said. She could not help feeling agitated. She was being accused of lying. 'Two paracetamol.'

'It can't have been just paracetamol. You can get that at Boots. Why would anyone ask the college nurse for it? Everyone knows you can give them things which help with exams.'

'Everyone knows wrong then,' said Imogen. 'A college nurse cannot give anything which requires a prescription. If it were not available from Boots, in fact, it would not be available from me. At any time when exams are in prospect we are doubly careful, in case someone should feel slowed down by some medication, and not do their best. I have never heard of anyone claiming to have been stimulated by medication so as to out-perform their best.'

The Senior Tutor cleared his throat, and said, 'Miss Quy, may we take it that there is no possibility of mistake? That you are morally certain that you could not have given any other drug on this occasion?'

Imogen paused. She thought very carefully. 'I cannot actually remember giving Mr Framingham any pills. It is not surprising I can't remember – I am consulted many times a week all term, and many dozens of times in the run-up to exams. That is why I keep a register of every single pill given out. Now that the question has arisen, I am resting my answers on two things – first the entry in the book –' She brought the book out of her bag, and put it on the table, 'and second the very fact that I don't remember the occasion. For me to have given any very potent medication to Mr Framingham or anyone else would be unprecedented – I could not possibly have done such a thing and then forgotten about it. Indeed I could not possibly have done such a thing at all.'

Framingham's tutor asked, 'Is there any possibility that you intended to dispense paracetamol, but actually inadvertently gave something else? You are not a qualified dispensing pharmacist.'

'No,' said Imogen, 'indeed not. That is one powerful reason why it would be wrong for me to dispense prescription medicines to undergraduates. But the sort of mistake you ask me about could not occur – or rather could not occur without being discovered. We run a kind of double-entry book-keeping. Amounts of medicines purchased are entered here –' she showed them a page of the register – 'amounts given out are entered here – and we have a regular audit of the medicine cupboard to make sure that amounts tally with the amounts in the book. Any discrepancy would cause an investigation at once.'

'Miss Quy,' the tutor said, 'can we be quite sure that paracetamol is incapable of causing an exceptionally fine performance? The lay public is often told that individual reactions to drugs are varied and somewhat unpredictable.'

'I am not a pharmacologist,' said Imogen. 'I can only say that in all my training and all my scope of experience I have never heard of any such effect being reported. As far as I know paracetamol is an analgesic, pure and simple.'

'Thank you Miss Quy,' said the tutor, and she stood down.

Framingham's tutor was summing up. He asked the Court to have due regard to the terrible consequences for his pupil of being found guilty. Not only would he be deprived of his degree, and sent down from Cambridge at once; he would have very great difficulty getting any kind of job with a reputation for cheating hung round his neck ... Surely the Court should be exceptionally certain of the case against him before making such a finding. And there was some room for doubt . . .

Not much though. By and by the Court retired into private session, and Imogen left. She retreated to her office in college, taking her dispensing book with her, and carefully replacing it in her filing cabinet. She locked the filing drawer, having realised how crucial the book was.

When, later, she was leaving college for the day she walked into an aftermath. A trunk and a pile of gear with a bicycle propped up against it was stacked in the porch. Framingham was leaning against the gateway arch, head down. As Imogen stepped past him he suddenly began to shout at her.

'Bitch!' he cried. 'Bloody unfeeling bitch! You could have got me out of this; just one word from you would have given me the benefit of the doubt! What did it matter to you? You could have helped me, you bloody self-protecting hellcat, you cow!'

Imogen stopped in her tracks, stunned. The head porter arrived, shooting out of his glass-fronted booth like an avenging angel in a bowler hat, but before he got there a couple of passing students had lifted Framingham bodily out of the college on to the pavement, where his taxi to the station was just pulling up to the kerb. Several pairs of hands helped his luggage away with him.

14

'You are shaking Miss Quy. Let me help you. Let me take you to the
Combination Room and sit you down with a drink.' The speaker was
Dr Bagadeuce, St Agatha's Fellow in Mathematics. Imogen realised
that she was indeed trembling, though whether it was with anger or
not she hardly knew. She never recalled being the object of such
hatred before in her entire life. She let Dr Bagadeuce accompany
her to the Combination Room, and pour her a whisky – it would be
silly to try to ride her bicycle home when feeling so agitated.

'What a contemptible lout he is,' said Bagadeuce. 'You must try
to ignore him. He richly deserves his fate.'

'I suppose he does; if we are all quite sure . . .'

'He's done it before, you know.'

'Done it before?'

'Cheating. It's addictive. Or rather, it is when you get away with
it. He was in trouble over his A level papers. The exam syndics gave
him the benefit of the doubt.'

'What was wrong with his A levels?' Imogen asked.

'A couple of folded pages. Crucial pages.'

'Did the Court of Discipline know that?'

'Oh, no. We try to proceed fairly. In a court of law, as you know,
a previous record is inadmissible; and this one was a doubt, not a
certainty. He would have cried persecution all the way to the Court
of Human Rights in Strasbourg . . . In the Middle Ages we could
have tarred and feathered him, and quite right too!'

Imogen was rapidly getting over her own trauma, and focusing her
attention on her companion. Surely that last remark was a little over
the top? He must have seen her looking at him curiously, for he said,
'Some of us love the college, Miss Quy, and serve it all òur lives. To
see its good name dragged in the mud . . .'

Imogen looked up sharply. His face was set. She thought he might
not be joking. 'Surely nobody will blame the college?' she said, gently.
'Such an action is a personal one, nothing to do with anything any

other member of college has done or not done. Neither his supervisor nor his tutor could have known what he was thinking of doing . . .'

'I suppose you are right,' he said. 'In these dishonourable days such crimes are quickly forgotten. And at least, this time, it was only a junior member of college . . .'

'This time?' said Imogen in astonishment, whereupon Dr Bagadeuce coloured slightly, and bit his lip. Then he said, 'I hope you are sufficiently recovered? It is getting rather late.'

'I'm fine now,' she told him. 'Thank you for your kindness.'

Whereupon he got up and left.

'This time?' Imogen thought. *'When was the last time?'* But she was weary of thinking about cheating. She finished her drink and went home, pushing her bike rather than riding it through the dusk.

The house when she reached it was empty and dark. No lights on in the upstairs flat, no friendly elephantine footfalls, or tuneless singing drifting down the stairwell. The tenants Imogen had to keep loneliness at bay, even the well-loved Fran, were an uncertain quantity. Of course, Fran was away; Imogen could have gone too if it had not been for the wretched Court of Discipline. Imogen lit the fire, and then put the kettle on. She picked the freesheet off the doormat, and sat down with it at the breakfast-room table with her cup of tea. There was a knock at the door. Imogen got up reluctantly, and opened it to Josh.

'Oh, come in Josh. I've just made a cup of tea. How do you like it?'

'With no tea, sugar or milk, and lots of gin and tonic,' he said grinning.

'Cadge,' she said. 'Rotter. Why do I put up with you?'

'We have a lot in common,' he said.

'Oh? What's that, then? Ice?'

'Yes please. We are both devoted to Fran. Me in a predatory, and you in a maternal mode.' He sat himself in the battered armchair. 'And talking of Fran, I dropped in to ask you if she happened to mention to you when she would be back from the goose chase.'

'No,' said Imogen, frowning as she tried to remember. 'No, she didn't. She asked me to go with her, and she mentioned a few days, but I didn't think to ask how many were a few. Didn't she tell you?'

'She said she didn't know how long it would take.'

'How long what would take? Did you say wild goose chase?'

'Yes I did. She was looking for a village in Wales.'

'Which village in Wales?'

'She didn't know. The one in which the cursed Summerfield spent a few days in 1978.'

'What made her think he went somewhere in Wales?'

'That Melanie had a dim recollection that it might have been . . .'

'Josh, how in heaven's name did she mean to find which village? Did she have some clues?'

'She was going to drive around in her father's car, borrowed for the occasion, and scrabble around in hotel registers . . .'

'I shouldn't think hotels keep their registers that long . . . But surely we can just ask Bullion père how long he lent the car for?'

'He's abroad for three months. That's why the car was available.'

'Well, she left the day before yesterday. She had to pick up the car . . . It's early to be worrying yet, Josh.'

'Oh, I'm not worrying yet. I'm just wondering when I should start to worry. Well, the truth is, I thought she might have phoned.'

'I would have thought she might have phoned you,' said Imogen. 'I wouldn't have expected her to phone me.'

'Well, the truth is . . .' said Josh. He was looking very unhappy. 'We had a little spat just before she left. So she might not phone me while she's still feeling cross. And the longer it takes her to find her village in Wales the crosser she might get . . . I wish she would phone. Or come back. I hate being cross. I want to make it up with her.'

Imogen looked at him sympathetically. Of course he didn't like being separated from Fran in the middle of a quarrel; she could remember only too well what such tribulations felt like when one was young . . .

'What was the spat about, Josh?' she asked. 'Was it serious?'

'Not at all. Perfectly stupid. I just suggested that the trip was ridiculous. Over the top. Unlikely in the extreme to be worth it. Impossible. You get the idea. I said I would go with her to the ends of the earth if the end in question had a grid reference. Was precisely specified. I would go with her to any particular village in Wales. But not to an unspecified one . . . She told me to please myself, and left.'

'Hmmph. More gin?'

'No thank you; too much is depressive rather than bracing. Look, could I ask you – would you let me know if she writes, phones, returns to base?'

'Certainly. Would you do the same for me?'

'I haven't got you worrying now? You always seem so sensible . . .'

'Like you, I'm not worried yet. And the sensible demeanour is a cunning disguise. Designed to conceal a tender heart, a paranoid tendency and insane ambition to be beloved of all who know me . . .'

Josh laughed, and gave her a peck on the cheek as he left.

Those who worry, of course, do so most in the small hours. Imogen lay awake, thinking. Fran was such a sensible girl, really, in spite of her wild enthusiasms, and passionate statements of principle. She was just what a sensible but not insensitive person *would* be when young. Could she really be scouring Wales without any clues at all to where to look? Imogen concluded that something somebody had said to Fran must have offered a clue. Wales, after all, was an extensive principality. Bitterly she resented the Court of Discipline which had prevented her from going with Fran; Fran would have confided in her, and they would have been pleasantly occupied in the quest together. That wretched boy! Cheating is a miserable sort of crime, Imogen reflected, and an odd one; not like straightforward theft or GBH. The most likely victim of such a crime is the perpetrator himself. Or herself, of course.

Unavoidably now, as she lay sleepless, she was turning over the cheating incident in her mind. Had she been right to assert so categorically that paracetamol could not possibly give someone a high? What if it had that effect in combination with other things – the boy might have been taking other things? Sighing, resigning herself to her own inability to forget it and get some sleep, Imogen got up, put on her faded tartan dressing-gown and her sheepskin slippers, and plodded downstairs.

The Family Medical dictionary confirmed her in what she had said to the Court. It did not mention interactions, malign or otherwise. Imogen went through to the kitchen, and helped herself to a stack of three chocolate digestives, and a glass of milk. The house felt forlorn. She *hated* living in an empty house. And how silly she was being! If Fran had been there, the house would still have been dark and silent at this hour, and Imogen would not have considered waking her up to chat! But then if Fran had been there, Imogen would probably have been fast asleep herself.

Still cross with herself, Imogen went into the spare room, and hauled out from the bottom drawer of a chest of drawers a battered cardboard folder containing her notes on toxicology, made during her nursing training. Below the familiar folder was another – labelled 'Old notes on Tox'. It came from Imogen's years of training as a doctor, before she abandoned her career for love . . . She took both files downstairs, and lit the gas fire to sit beside. The American clock that her father had so loved ticked encouragingly in the quiet room, counting while the fire steadily hissed. An owl hooted a little way off; it must be hunting in the trees along the river bank.

'Poor mouse,' thought Imogen.

There was very little about paracetamol in Imogen's nursing notes – or at least very little except recommendations of it as a pain killer, all the way from arthritis to z-plasty. She turned to the other folder, and pulled out a stack of sheets of paper, written over in a handwriting that no longer looked like her own. Aconite, antiseptics, barbiturates, DNOC . . . Imogen was about to turn the page. DNOC. Weedkiller and insecticide. At one time used to treat obesity. Absorption through the skin, as well as by injection or inhalation . . . initial feelings of well-being, followed by fatigue, thirst, hyperpyrexia, convulsions, coma and death . . .

Imogen read this entry several times, and then went, thoughtful, back to bed, where paradoxically she fell asleep at once.

15

In Imogen's life housework was an activity of last resort. She did quite a lot of it, because she hated living in an untidy house. The last resort was resorted to quite often, in fact. Hoovering the stairs was the very worst job – quite hard work, involving heaving the heavy vacuum cleaner up and down three flights, and clumsy – the damn thing wouldn't stand on a stair while you used it, being just too large and heavy . . . and in a mistaken fit of design consciousness, Imogen had chosen a plain stair-carpet in soft moss green, which showed every speck of either light or dark coloured dirt. Fran's few days in Wales had now extended to five, without a phone call to Josh, and Imogen was wrestling with the vacuum cleaner, and wondering why all dirt was always either lighter or darker than the surface it fell upon . . . She started at the top of the stairs, and while she was up there Hoovered Fran's rugs, and then worked her way down, slightly out of breath, and miserable, and cross.

Dust accumulated on the white-painted woodwork, the moulding of the angled skirting boards that ran down beside the stairs, between the turned banister rails, on every pleasant detail of the Victorian house. Imogen ran the snout of the vacuum cleaner over the paintwork, which was quicker than using a duster, and nearly as efficient. Towards the bottom of the stairs, when she had worked her way backwards almost into the hall, there was a little fragment of paper sitting on the skirting among the dust. Imogen zapped it with the crevice-cleaner tool on the end of the cleaner hose. It stayed put. She tried again, and then realised it was not a tiny piece of paper irresistibly stuck to the base of the wall, but the corner of a larger piece that had fallen behind the skirting, and was protruding by a bare quarter inch. She tried to ease it out, gripping it by her finger nail, but she couldn't do it. She put the vacuum cleaner down, and went to her work-box for a pair of tweezers.

It was a postcard, or something. The skirting board had parted from the wallplaster by a quarter inch or so – such are the ways of old houses – and whatever it was had slipped into the gap. Not a postcard – a photograph. A scuffed, creased photograph with battered corners, a greyish black-and-white print. It showed a group of people leaning against a farm gate. They were very small – there was a lot of background. A man with string round his trousers below the knees, holding a hayfork; a young woman in a print dress and wellington boots, and a man in an open-necked shirt and flannels, hands in pockets, standing between the two. Imogen sat on the bottom stair, smoothing the picture and staring at it. At first she couldn't imagine who it was – friends of her parents? But although she didn't Hoover often, the picture surely couldn't have been there that long! In fact how could it have got there? Imogen recollected the papers bursting out of the box in the arms of the delivery man, and falling everywhere in the hall – fluttering through the banisters, skithering down the wall . . . this photo, presumably, lodging unnoticed in the crack between plaster and woodwork . . . Perhaps the corner had been lifted into view by the noisy suck of the crevice nozzle just a moment ago.

The picture might have – must have – come from the Summerfield papers. The smiling young man was the great Gideon. But Imogen's first thought had been that the photo belonged in the dress box upstairs, on top of her wardrobe – the box full of ancient snapshots taken on dozens of annual holidays on her father's box brownie and its successor simple cameras; and she had thought this because of the familiar, well-loved outline of the mountain in the distance, behind the field-gate with its three figures. Imogen could say within half a mile where the picture had been taken; she had spent her childhood holidays roaming around the Tanat valley while her father fished, and her mother snoozed in a deck chair in the farmhouse garden, her knitting neglected on her lap.

Stamping on the spiralling mist of recollection, Imogen spelled it out to herself. She was possibly looking at evidence of where Summerfield spent the missing month in the long-ago summer. Very probably, really, when you took into account that Fran had never mentioned Wales in connection with him, and yet the picture proved he had been there at least once. Could it be coincidence that Fran had suddenly decided to depart for Wales, and – awful thought – was it coincidence that she had been gone longer than expected? Imogen felt suddenly sick. What could she do? Who could she talk to? Whose help would be any good? Josh? Mike?

Josh first – he might know something.

As it happened, he didn't. He should have asked Fran if she had any clue to help her in searching the principality, and he hadn't.

'You see, she couldn't have seen this –' said Imogen, waving the photograph. 'So if she did have a lead it was something else.'

Josh shook his head. 'I just don't know,' he said. 'But it feels all wrong. She's not vindictive – usually we make things up in a few hours. I really thought she would have rung me by now . . .'

Imogen put in her hours at the College, and then went to see Mike. They showed her into his office, where the filing cabinets towered above and around him, and a glass screen offered precarious privacy from the next-door office. Mike shared the tiny space with an officer called Robinson who looked up, nodded briefly, and went back to his form-filling.

'People don't get to be missing persons until they're most definitely missing,' said Mike, when Imogen had told him her story. 'But I don't like the feel of this much; not in the light of what you tell me, and what you say about other biographers of this chap. Even so, most likely she's just happily perusing her researches, or she's even on her way home right now.'

'There's only one hotel in the valley,' Imogen told him. 'And the pub. But there are dozens and dozens of people doing bed and breakfast. The local policeman . . .'

'What powers you credit me with!' said Mike. 'I don't know any of the many thousands of policemen in Wales. But all right, I'll see what informal channels might reveal. Satisfied?'

'Too worried,' said Imogen, smiling at him wanly. 'But grateful.'

Imogen knew, really, that she would have to go herself. She would have to drive herself there, put up in the pub, ask questions, discover if Fran had been, or was still, in the valley. If nothing was wrong she would find Fran easily, and Fran would be furious with her; the last row would be nothing compared to the fury that would be visited on a landlady who followed her tenants around, leaning on them worse than the bossiest and most impossible parent . . . but until she did something about it she wasn't going to sleep at nights. Why hadn't she panicked at once, and gone in pursuit earlier? The mere fact that earlier there hadn't yet been enough rational cause for alarm didn't in the least convince her now.

She set about preparing to go. She told the bursar of St Agatha's that she was taking a few days' leave, and arranged with her semi-retired friend Mary to work her college hours for her – after all it was full term. She told Lady B. what she was doing. She told Shirl and Pansy that she would miss the next sewing session; she cancelled the milk. She packed a suitcase, locked the back door, and opened the front door to carry her case to her car, which lived parked outside the front garden, under a street light. Mike was standing at her gate.

'I rather thought you might,' he said. 'I wish you wouldn't.'

'How can there be no good cause for alarm about Fran, and any cause to worry about me?' Imogen asked him crisply.

'I didn't come to argue,' he said. 'I'm on my way home for my grub. I came to tell you she isn't in the hotel or the pub, and that PC Emlyn Jones is on the lookout for her or anyone answering her description. OK?'

Imogen could almost feel pallor spreading over her cheeks. So long as every responsible adult around her was refusing to take the thing seriously she could calmly with the upper part of her mind regard it as an internal truth only; something that was in a way a game of her own. If Mike was suddenly listening to her then with a leap the sense of danger sprang nearer.

'There isn't a law against going to Wales,' Imogen said, trying for her usual robustly independent tone.

'Story of my life, that,' said Mike. 'When anyone wants a bit of unofficial help it's oh, Mike, dear Mike, couldn't you just, Mike? And the next minute it's the letter of the law and my advice isn't wanted, thank you very much. Just make sure you phone me every day, my girl, or I'll have PC Emlyn Jones after you like a flash, law or no law. Got it?'

'Mike, I'm very sorry, I didn't mean . . .' she said, but he was stomping away down the pavement back to his car, saying 'hmmph!' over his shoulder. He grinned at her over the open driver's door as he got in, and waved.

Suddenly sure that if she didn't go at once she might think better of it, Imogen swung her case on to the back seat, ran back to check that she had locked the front door, and drove herself away.

* * *

She didn't like motorways. England spooled past her windscreen, looking for many miles almost as she remembered it from long ago. It had always been a long journey from Cambridge. She had set out with her mother and father, thermos flask propped in a wicker basket, rugs tucked round their knees, luggage roped to a roofrack that whistled in the wind as they drove, the road atlas – a pre-war job bound in crumbling leather, open on her mother's lap. She was always car-sick. The remembered nausea was the one thing she didn't regret in the memories – car-sickness had disappeared for good when she learned to drive.

West of Cambridge the landscape is self-effacing and gentle. The church spires rise from the trees which cluster in the villages, having been banished from the sweeping gentle undulations of the vast open fields. The chalky pallor of the ploughed and combed soils shows off the almost fluorescent green of the winter wheat. The skies were full of little woolly clouds, as though the heavens regretted the lack of earthly sheep . . . Of course, something was wrong; less birdsong, fewer wild flowers in the verges than she remembered; Milton Keynes had once been nothing but fields, a mere name on a signpost; and the A5, while no doubt becoming safer, was losing the quality of the great Telford road that swept through England and Wales to Holyhead; the little toll-houses standing mud-spattered and forlorn on one side or the other of the dualled and thundering roadways. Further along the road the landscape changed, the western configurations of hill and farms, less crop, more livestock, less anxious churches content with modest towers among the surrounding hills. Imogen was soothed. This quiet land of village and green and pub, this landscape cultivated in several senses, was a gentle law-abiding place in which, surely, hardly anything ever really happened, and serial murder was diminishingly rare.

She stopped in Shrewsbury, and found a pub supper, and was quite startled to find the conversation in the bar all about cattle rustling. Peaceful appearances could be deceptive anywhere, it seemed. What was that Housman poem her father used to quote?

> *High the vanes of Shrewsbury gleam*
> *Islanded in Severn Stream*
> *The bridges from the steepled crest*
> *Cross the water east and west.*

Jill Paton Walsh

The flag of Morn, in conqueror's state,
Enters at the English gate.
The vanquished eve as night prevails,
Bleeds upon the road to Wales.

And indeed she drove on into a spectacular conflagration that made driving difficult as the setting sun blinded westbound drivers. At Oswestry she stopped for the night. The bed-and-breakfast place she remembered from so long ago was still in business with quite different owners, just as shabby and comfortable as before. Imogen fended off night-thoughts by sitting in the family living-room, watching television with the grandparents until she could hardly keep her eyes open.

16

The valley was entirely familiar, deeply etched on Imogen's younger mind. She had both remembered, and forgotten it. What she had remembered was the appearance of the valley, and the mountainside, the stout, four-square houses, the Methodist chapels painted black and white, the tumbling river winding noisily along the valley floor, the very shapes of the shadows cast across the road by the looming heights that made up the southern wall of the valley. This escarpment stood permanently in the light, its steep north-facing sides dark all day long, all year round. What she had forgotten was how she felt about the place; the tension between pleasure at the beauty, and claustrophobia; how could people bear to live on the shadowy side of the valley?

She was sharply aware of why she had never, since her parent's death, returned here. And yet she had been happy here as a child. At the head of the valley the road wound over the pass to Vyrnwy, and the village came into view. Wildly unexpected, the little terrace rows of Victorian houses stood on the hillside in stripes, as though a thoughtless child had left his toys scattered. No rural beauty; above the rows of houses the slate quarry left the gouged and broken holes and mounds of spoil heaps, grey in sunlight, navy-blue in rain. And here was the pub where, Imogen remembered, flinching, from her adolescence, the language at the bar changed from English to Welsh as a stranger entered, and changed back again as they rose to leave.

She had a little trouble finding the farm she had stayed in as a child. The road had been straightened at the foot of the mountain, and the well-remembered hair-raising bends had become milder. By and by she found her way. The farmyard was as muddy and richly odorous as ever, and a pleasant young woman was working, feeding the pigs, who crowded along the trough outside the sties. An old horse looked over his stable-door, and harrumphed.

'I'm very sorry,' she said, smiling at Imogen. 'But there's no bed and breakfast here now. You would find somewhere in the village, easy.'

'I'm an old guest here,' said Imogen. 'My name is Quy, Imogen Quy. My parents used to spend every summer here . . .'

'Why, goodness!' said the woman. 'Imo, is it? Don't you remember me? I'm Gwenny!'

'Gwenny! – Heavens, Gwenny!' said Imogen, astonished. Gwenny had been a little, bird-boned creature, scampering everywhere – and now she was a tall, hefty, muscular figure, with bronzed arms, and stout, reddened working hands.

'You will have tea, now,' said Gwenny firmly, leading Imogen indoors.

The farmhouse was changed considerably less than Gwenny. Dark and cool, with low beams, a deep window-seat in the mullioned window bay, covered in tatty cushions, and bearing a sleeping dog at one end, and a sleeping cat at the other. The floor was made of great slabs of local slate. An iron range filled the huge chimney nook, with five doors shut on the ovens, and one open to flood the room with warmth from the fire. In front of the fire Gwenny's dad sat rocking in his elaborate old chair, reading a newspaper. His slippered feet were propped on another sleeping dog.

'Look who's here, Dad,' said Gwenny. 'Do you remember Imo?'

The old man looked at Imogen steadily with watery eyes. Then he heaved himself up from his chair, and reached for a photograph from the mantelpiece. He handed it to Imogen, who found herself looking at a picture of herself in a cotton sunhat, no more than three feet tall, throwing hay in the air with a tiny garden fork. Behind her rows of men worked with real hayforks, her father one of them. Memory flooded back to her, bringing the scent of hay, and the smart of sunburn on her back. The crossed straps of her summer dress had been stamped on her painful skin in white, she remembered . . .

Gwenny took the simmering iron kettle from a hot ring, and was already wetting the tea.

'We thought you would be coming back,' the old farmer said, replacing the photograph between a studio portrait of his dead wife, and a snapshot of a prize-winning pig, with a ribbon from the Oswestry show pinned to the frame. 'Long enough, you've been about it.' He regarded her critically. 'You have a good colour for a city lass,' he said. 'None of that pasty look, I'm glad to see.'

Gwenny put up an ancient little gate-legged table, and spread a white cloth over it. A stout brown teapot accompanied bone china cups, delicate and pretty. Flapjacks and scones and jam were set out, before Gwenny announced 'elevenses' but the old man grumbled bitterly at the absence of gingerbread. 'Not a patch on your mother at the housekeeping, Gwenny,' he said.

Imogen sat in the chair brought up for her, and tried not to eat too much of the elevenses. She and Gwenny had serious talking to do. Little by little she led the talk round to Fran.

'No,' said Gwenny. 'No, I haven't heard of anyone just recently. Dad? There hasn't been anyone in the valley, isn't it?'

'There might've been someone at the Doctor's, Gwenny,' he said.

'True enough. There's a doctor has the old cowman's cottage, down the English road a bit – you remember, Imo, where old Williams used to live – he has people staying with him, and nobody knows about it unless they come up to the shop, or a meal in the Fisherman's Rest. But there – the doctor is from Cambridge, Dad; Imo will know all about him and his friends. There's nowhere else could have a stranger staying without we knew all about it, Imo, except perhaps in August when it's people by the three dozen coming here. It will be some other valley she's in.'

'She would be looking for somewhere where someone might remember a holiday maker from long ago. Someone called Dr Summerfield. The name doesn't ring a bell with you, Gwenny?'

'Dr Summerfield? No. Sorry, Imo. Unless – a lady doctor, is it? There's someone comes bothering the Evanses now and then.'

'I wonder if she's anyone I know?'

'She wouldn't be a friend of yours, Imo, she's a menace, so she is. An antique dealer lady. She won't take no for an answer, but pesters, and pesters, and keeps coming back. Harassing people . . .'

'Well, the one I'm thinking of isn't an antique dealer. Has this person been harassing you, Gwenny?'

'Not me. Evans. Up at Quarry Farm. Over and over.'

'Funny you should mention Quarry Farm,' said Imogen, producing the battered photograph from her bag. 'Where would you think this was taken, Gwenny? Up that way somewhere, I should think. It might be a clue to what my friend Fran is looking for.'

'That's the gate to Evans' three acre top field,' said Gwenny without hesitating. 'And there won't be any English up there, Imo. They won't have them set foot on their land. Funny, that,' she added, sipping her tea, 'when you think that old Granny Evans was English. Wasn't she, Dad?'

'Old David Evans took his sheep down to Shrewsbury Fair just after the war, and came back with a wife,' said the old man. 'Talk of the valley, it was. She couldn't speak a word of the language, and the Evans hadn't a word of English.'

'How did she manage?' asked Imogen.

'She learned,' he said. 'That was a fine woman. Gone now,' he sighed. 'She could *swear* in Welsh, something frightful!' he said, grinning. 'What a trimegant! The Evanses were all chapel, and she was Church. She'd have the pony trap every Sunday, and gallivant off to church, and all the rest of the family would have to walk to chapel. Talk of the valley, in her day . . .'

He meandered off into recollection of his youth.

Imogen realised that when he had described a wife brought into the valley 'just after the war' he had meant the First World War. He would have gone on all day, wool-gathering, lost in recollection, but she gently extricated herself after an hour.

Gwenny walked with her to the gate.

'I would make up a bed for you, and you could stay here, where you belong,' she offered, but Imogen could see that one pair of hands would be overworked already, without guests.

'Thank you, Gwenny, but I'm booked in at the Inn,' she said.

'I hope they air the sheets down there,' said Gwenny suspiciously. 'You'll catch a chill . . .'

'I'll be fine!' said Imogen. 'Gwenny, you don't happen to know the name of the Doctor who has Williams' cottage now?'

'Funny, but I don't,' said Gwenny. 'He gets called "Happy Chappy", or "The English" mostly. I haven't ever seen him myself. He isn't here much.

'You know what rich English are like, buying the place up to use it like a holiday camp . . . Happy Chappy, that's what he's called. I hope you find your friend, Imo.

'And don't go home without coming for another cuppa, will you? Makes a change for Dad. He likes to talk to people.'

17

It came on to rain in the afternoon. Imogen looked in the boot of her car for warm waterproof clothing. She found a good Aran sweater, one she had knitted herself long ago, and her bicycle cape – capacious and hooded. She was going to look like a walking tent wearing these, but what was the point of vanity so far from home? She left the car pulled off on the verge of the main road, and began to tramp up the muddy track to Quarry Farm. What was it, she wondered as she walked, the ladies of Cranford had said? What was the point of vanity at home, where everybody knows us? And what was the point of vanity in 'town where nobody knows us? Something like that.

The Evanses had certainly barricaded their farm. A sequence of gates across the track as it rose up the valley side were padlocked, and crested with spirals of barbed wire. Warning notices decorated the stiles. NO ENTRY. TRESPASSERS WILL BE PROSECUTED. KEEP OUT. VISITORS BY EXPRESS APPOINTMENT ONLY. DANGER – SHOOTING. WARNING – FIERCE DOGS AT LARGE. These signs would have been more alarming had each one not been accompanied by another, saying, in Welsh, 'Come on up'.

It was Imogen's smattering of Welsh that led to her not taking the signs seriously enough. She could see the farm, snuggled into the mountainside some way above her, a dozen trees planted round it for shelter, its barns and yard between her and the house. She doggedly climbed the stiles, and ignored the notices. When she had still a quarter of a mile or so to go she heard a shout, far off. She stopped and looked around. A man was standing at the entrance to the farmyard, looking down the track towards her and shouting. She waved and continued towards the last gate.

When he fired his gun she stopped. He had not aimed at her; just discharged the thing into the air. He was shouting again. She cupped her hands around her mouth, and yelled back, 'I need to talk to you!'

'Get out!' he was yelling. 'You'll be sorry! Get out!'

Imogen tried shouting *'Boro da!'* but it's hard to sound inoffensive and friendly when calling across another mountainside at a distance of a quarter of a mile. She took a few uncertain steps forward, and then she saw the dogs. Not the familiar black-and-white sheep dogs, with their narrow sharp-eyed faces, and harmless barking at strangers; these were huge black dogs, of uncertain breed. The man had let them out of the barn – the door was standing wide now – and they were hurtling downhill towards her. Imogen's courage failed her, and she turned and ran.

It was only a few paces back to the last stile; Imogen would have made it, even encumbered by her flapping cycle cape, if she hadn't tripped and fallen. She caught her foot in a hummock of grass and went flying. The wrench shot daggers of pain through her ankle – she heard the bone snap – and then the dogs were upon her. One of them sunk its teeth in her forearm, snarling and dragging at her – the other had got a grip on her cape and was tearing at it and snarling. Terrified, and in agony, trying to wrap her face in her free arm, Imogen heard human cries, and a sequence of high-pitched whistles. The dogs released her arm and clothing and raced away. She tried to sit up, and fainted.

When she came to she was being carried. Someone had hold of her by her armpits, and someone else by the knees, walking between her legs. Every step jolted her painfully. Her left hand was warm and sticky. The two who were carrying her were talking together – urgent, agitated voices, rather short of breath, presumably from the effort of carrying her uphill.

'Mother will kill you for this, Daffyd!' said the voice at her head.

'I didn't know, see! I thought it was *her!*' said the other. Then one of them stumbled, and the flash of pain in her leg was followed by oblivion.

It felt like a long time later when she came round again. She was propped on a sofa, in a dark, warm kitchen with a huge old range, and battered table and chairs very like Gwenny's. Her leg was up on the sofa, held between cushions. Her arm was dangling, her hand immersed in a bowl of warm blood. She frowned down at this ghoulish sight, and finally worked out that it was a bowl of warm water, into which her arm was steadily bleeding.

The same voice as before was saying, 'I thought it was *her*, see!'

'But it's a little, thin woman she is!' said a woman's voice, crossly.

'She was wearing a cape sort of thing, mother. Made her look large enough . . .'

'We are in trouble now, right enough, whatever she looked like! What are we to do with her now?' said 'mother'.

'Phone Gwenny Floyd, and ask her to come and fetch me,' said Imogen. Immediately she had spoken she felt a heaving sensation, and leaning over her bloody bowl she was very sick.

'You are a friend of Gwenny's is it?' said the woman. She was almost crying with vexation. 'Whatever will people think about us? There's crazy, those boys are!'

Imogen was beginning to shiver violently. Her teeth rattled together in her head. She looked at her ankle, which was aching in a somehow sinister way, and saw that it was thick and swollen. She was going to need a doctor. A high-pitched humming sound was ringing in her ears – someone had left a untuned radio set on, and she wondered why they didn't turn it off.

The cross woman brought her a clean bowl of warm water, and then a cup of tea, and a warm wet towel. Imogen shook her head.

'Sip it and you'll feel a little better, my dear,' she said.

'I need a doctor,' said Imogen.

'Help is coming, don't you worry,' the woman said.

'Have you got a bandage?' asked Imogen faintly. 'My arm is bleeding.'

'I'll bind it up for you in a minute,' the woman said. 'But better let bites bleed for a little first . . .'

She could be right, Imogen thought. A flow of blood being the best way to clean a deep puncture like a dog bite . . . The hot sweet tea was right for shock too, though not if she was going to need an anaesthetic. She was woozing gently, in and out of consciousness perhaps. It occurred to her that the high-pitched hum was in her own head.

It was later again. There were voices around her.

'. . . and to cap it all, she's a friend of Gwenny's' – that was 'mother' who sounded so cross with her menfolk, and so kind to Imogen. 'Whatever am I going to say to Gwenny?'

Then a new voice, saying, 'Just thank your lucky stars, Mrs Owen, that it isn't worse. I'll be able to make her comfortable. The problem is the bites. She will need a tetanus injection right away—'

'My tetanus protection is up to date,' said Imogen.

'Ho, ho, a sensible woman, and wide awake, I see,' the doctor said. 'Good, good. In that case we don't need to move you. Now, I'm going to put a splint on your tibia, and I have to get it quite straight first. So just a little painkiller . . .' He produced a surprisingly large syringe with a little clear liquid in it. Imogen flinched at the sight of it, and then braced herself – how often had she silently accused a patient of cowardice? Very gently and efficiently he emptied the syringe into her uninjured arm, and she slid into peaceful and total oblivion.

She awoke in a very large bed, under a sloping ceiling. A hefty oak chest of drawers stood against the wall on her left, with a mirror hanging behind it. The bedside table was adorned with a lace mat, and had a tea tray on it, with a cup of tea standing in its saucer. Imogen could see it was cold without moving to touch it – it had a brown scummy surface. The sun was pouring through the window in the dormer and it was already late – the light had the brightness of mid-morning. Very gingerly Imogen tried to move – first her arm, which she at once felt was bandaged. It was sore, and the bottom of the bandage was anchored round her thumb, but all her fingers moved freely, and it didn't hurt too much. Even more carefully she tried moving her leg. There was a splint on it below the knee, and it hurt enough to make her stop. She looked at the ceiling for a while, and then moving very slowly, shifted herself up on to the pillows a bit, so that she could see round the room. At once her attention was drawn to the patchwork quilt under which she was lying.

It entirely covered the huge bed. It was in soft and faded colours – pinks, white, lilacs, blues, pale greens and browns. It had only two shapes – fat diamonds and skinny diamonds. Imogen stared at it appreciatively. 'Where's the repeat?' she wondered. As sleepiness ebbed away she looked more carefully. And she couldn't find it. She kept thinking there was an area where the pattern repeated, and then noticing that one or two pieces were different . . .

The quilt was a masterwork. It had no repeat; it could not have been made conveniently block by block; it had been sewn in a single mind-blowing piece, each little patch stitched to the whole. What Imogen kept seeing in the swirling kaleidoscope of colours and patterns – she could see no two pieces the same – was ghostly shapes, a sort of irregular seven-sided shape which appeared in the pattern, and disappeared the moment you looked closely. A ghostly heptagon – a non-repeating pattern . . . *What was it Fran had said?* Imogen sat up abruptly, ignoring the pain in her leg, her scalp prickling and her spine shivering. Suddenly she knew exactly

where Gideon Summerfield had spent his missing weeks of that long
ago August; she knew why that was a secret worth killing for.
And when you know why you know who. Or so Mike once said.

There was a knock on her door, and Mrs Evans came in, carrying
a tray. 'You don't look so bad, now,' Mrs Evans said. 'I brought you
breakfast in bed. And to explain . . .'

Imogen felt astonishingly eager for the breakfast. Thick creamy
porridge with sugar and milk; a rack of toast with butter and marmalade . . . a pot of tea.

'Let me guess,' she said cheerfully. 'You've had a lot of trouble with
someone trying to buy this quilt. Someone called Janet Summerfield,
right?'

Janet Summerfield had given them no peace. She had tried asking;
she had tried offering lots of money. She had tried threats, of the
'You'll be sorry . . .' kind. She had tried cheating. Well, they were
almost certain it was her doing – a woman had turned up saying she
was from a museum of textile arts in Nottingham, and trying to get
them to lend the quilt for an exhibition. But they were not foolish; they
had telephoned the tourist office in Nottingham asking for a number
for the Textile Arts Museum, and found that there wasn't one. Then
there were three break-ins to the farmhouse – all on market days,
when everyone was out of their houses, but Mrs Evans had hidden
the quilt by then; putting it away in the dower chest together with
her mother's jewellery whenever she went anywhere.

'The dower chest is too heavy to steal, see, Miss Quy, and it has a
hefty old lock on it too. The burglars had a try the third time they
came, but they only scarred the wood a bit.'

'Do call me Imo,' said Imogen. 'It's Gwenny's name for me.'

'In the end we told her we would set the dogs on her next time she
set foot up here,' said Mrs Evans. 'And she must have believed us;
she hasn't tried again for nearly four years now. I'm sorry our Hugh
thought you were her, truly I am. He isn't too bright, Miss . . . Imo.
And she gave him such a bad time, see, he's jumpy about her.'

'What did she do to him?'

'She locked him in her garage. Then she put a kidnapper's note
through the door here, saying he'd be safe if the quilt was put in
a binbag beside the road, after dark. Silly, it was. Everyone knew
where he would be if she had got him; there's only the one garage
in the valley with a door that locks. And there's only her that's batty

about the quilt, see? PC Jones went and got our Hugh back, easy. She hadn't been cruel, mind; he had blankets, and plenty of food in there. But he was frightened.'

'Naturally he was,' said Imogen.

'So when he saw you coming he thought you were after him . . .'

'Don't worry about it,' said Imogen. 'It was a mistake. It's forgotten about. Just tell me about the quilt. Who made it?'

'Granny Vi made it. The house is full of quilts, Imo, but she always prided herself on this one. It's on the spare bed to keep it from too much wear, see.'

'It is magnificent,' said Imogen. 'And quite old, I imagine. Do you know when it was made?' But Imogen didn't need Holly's lecture to tell her that the quilt was older than Gideon Summerfield's precious piece of geometry.

'It must have been before the war. I can't remember the spare room without it,' said Mrs Evans. 'And I don't want to let it go, you see, not for ever so much money. She offered us five thousand pounds – *five thousand!* And Mr Evans would have taken it, just to get rid of her, but I wouldn't have it. It's my word goes inside the house, and his in the farmyard, so she didn't get it. And do you know, Imo, all the while, if I thought she liked it, I might have let her have it – goodness knows we could do with the money – but I didn't think she wanted it, somehow. She didn't look at it, like you were doing; how can you want a quilt you don't want to run your eyes over? There, I'm running on and on about it; you'll think we're all batty as owls in the valley.'

'No, I won't,' said Imogen. 'You sound perfectly sane to me. And you are quite right about Janet Summerfield. She doesn't want the quilt. She wants to destroy it. You must never let her have it.'

'Do you know her, then?' said Mrs Evans, eyeing Imogen curiously.

'I've met her. I'm just guessing what she would do with the quilt.'

'But your guess is the same as mine. I can see why Gwenny likes you. She'll be over to see you as soon as she can, by the way.'

'Did the doctor say I could get up?' asked Imogen.

'That wasn't the doctor. There isn't a doctor till Bala one way, and fifteen miles the other. That was the vet. I'll ring him and ask him.'

But just for now Imogen was glad to have the breakfast tray removed from her knees, and to wriggle down again into a comfortable position, and lie back against the pillows. She contemplated the quilt, timeworn into a state of exquisite delicacy, and wondered how it had been planned and sewn. In its Venetian frailty and beauty it seemed to her to be as much an object of desire and joy as an impressionist painting, or a Greek amphora.

18

The vet thought that if a cow could walk on a bone he had set, then a woman could. Although it was illegal for a doctor to treat a cow, it was perfectly legal for a vet to treat a woman; and as far as Imogen could tell the vet had been both kind and competent. Imogen got up, and made her way downstairs leaning on a borrowed walking stick. The question uppermost in her mind was Fran. She had been giving it careful thought. Fran had not seen the photograph that had, on her chance recognition of it, brought Imogen directly to the valley. She was at large somewhere in Wales, inspecting, or trying to inspect, ancient hotel registers. She would very obviously be in danger – perhaps great danger – if she turned up in this place, asking questions about Summerfield in 1978. Or rather, she would, if she did that, *and Janet Summerfield got to know*. So the first question was where was Janet Summerfield?

Imogen carefully sat herself down at the kitchen table, in the comfortable warmth of the range, and, she hoped, out of the way of Mrs Evans and her daughter, Megan, who were cooking. She leaned on her arm, and immediately stopped, wincing. She asked if either of the two women knew of any visitor to the valley – she was sure there would be a bush telegraph to tell them immediately if Janet Summerfield showed her face there.

They confidently denied all knowledge. Megan Evans had been serving at the hotel bar only last night, and helping in the dining-room. The place was very quiet, she said. Only a few fishermen, and without their wives. 'Wrong time of year for the crowds,' she told Imogen, putting a cup of tea in front of her.

Imogen embarked on a description of Fran. Had either of her hostesses seen or heard tell of anyone like that?

They shook their heads. Any English in the valley, they told her, would be at the Inn, or at Mrs Jones's, who did bed and breakfast, or at the Happy Chappy's cottage. Sometimes he lent it to people, or had friends staying. In summer, mostly. Someone in the village would have heard, they were sure, if anyone had arrived at the cottage. It always got around as soon as dusk fell – you could see the lights down the valley side from various windows in the village. People went to draw their curtains, and they saw at once if there was anyone in down there.

'You keep a watch on the Happy Chappy?' said Imogen, amused.

'Nothing much to do here, except gossip, see?' said Megan, ruefully. 'There's nothing against him.'

'Except he has funny friends,' said her mother.

'This friend of yours; would she have been driving a Rover? An old one? 3.5 litre coupé?' asked Megan.

'Golly, I don't know,' said Imogen, startled. 'I can recognise a Nova, because I drive one, but beyond that . . . and anyway, Fran borrowed her father's car; I never clapped eyes on it. What's a Rover whatdyecallit like?'

'It's women like you,' said Megan, 'that give the sex a bad name. That's a gorgeous car – and someone was driving one here the day before yesterday. I saw it parked in the Inn yard, with half the kids in the school gawking at it over the playground fence.'

'I just don't know what car she was driving,' said Imogen helplessly.

'If it was her,' said Megan, 'then she didn't stop long. Couple of hours, then it had gone.'

'I rather think that's a relief,' said Imogen. 'If harm comes to someone their car stays put . . .'

'There wouldn't be any harm would come to her, here!' said Mrs Evans, sounding shocked. 'There's hearts of gold they are here. Maybe we talk a bit about rich English, but there's no one would hurt a stranger . . .' She stopped in full flood, and flushed as she looked at Imogen, arm bandaged, leg stuck out stiffly splinted beside her chair.

Her embarrassment was cut short by a knock on the door. The new arrival entered without waiting. A policeman, taking off his helmet as he came in, and revealing a shock of carrot-red hair.

He greeted Mrs Evans and Megan with a flood of Welsh, and then turned to Imogen. 'Miss Quy, is it?'

Imogen admitted it.

'You've had a nasty experience, I hear,' he said. 'Sorry to hear that. Will you be thinking of making an official complaint?'

'No,' said Imogen. 'I will not. I have had an apology, and a good deal of care and kindness, and that will be that.'

He put away his notebook and pencil, and sat down at the kitchen table, tenderly putting his helmet down beside him, two-handed. 'How are you feeling, now?' he asked Imogen. 'Over the shock, are you?'

'More or less,' Imogen said.

A plate of scones, a dish of jam and a pot of tea had appeared beside the policeman as if by magic, and Megan and her mother retreated to the far end of the kitchen and busied themselves.

'I might have bad news for you, see,' the policeman said, demolishing a scone with two large bites. 'We have found a body. A woman's body.'

'Please – no!' said Imogen softly. A horrible feeling of dragging flow was spreading over her – face, guts, limbs, as though the shock had liquefied her and she was draining away.

'When did – the person – die?' she managed to ask at last.

'We don't know, see. Forensic are on their way. But we have some clothing and bits found with the body, and if you could manage to come down to the station with me and identify . . .'

'Yes,' said Imogen. The possibility of action, even such a ghastly action as that, galvanised her. She struggled to her feet, reaching for her stick.

The station was down the valley some way. PC Jones was gentle with Imogen, in a beefy sort of way. He sat her down at a battered wooden table in the back of the station, and offered to wait till a woman PC was available. Imogen said there was no need. He brought a large cardboard crate to the table, and took out of it a sequence of plastic bags, containing a biro, scraps of cloth, sodden fragments of a leather bound diary, a gold watch . . .

'Take your time,' he said. 'Look very carefully, if you please, at each item in turn . . .'

Imogen recognised none of it. With the watch she was quite certain; she had never seen Fran wearing that. Fran's watch was a jolly waterproof plastic thing with Minnie Mouse on the dial. Her relief was almost as debilitating as the shock of dread had been. She found herself trembling, laughing.

'None of this is hers,' she said.

'That's good then,' the policeman said. 'Good news for you, and for Miss Bullion's friends; bad news for someone else.'

He was visibly relaxing, and Imogen realised that he had been bracing himself to deal with her distress had any of the pitiful relics been Fran's. She warmed to him. 'Yes,' she said. 'Is it a case of foul play?'

'Yes indeed,' he told her. 'Very nasty blow to the back of the head.'

'And you can't say when?'

'The body was in a shallow grave in the peat, Miss Quy. Waterlogged ground. Up on the mountain. People always think the mountains will be dry, but they're soaking wet. Bogs all over them. And the peat preserves bodies nicely – been known to keep skin on the bones from the Iron Age till the present. It will take expert forensic to tell us when.'

'How did you find it?'

'Farmer was digging a channel through to dry it off a bit for his sheep.'

'I see.'

'Nobody is going to ask me,' he added, ruefully, 'And you don't like to claim to know, really, based on what happens to dead sheep – people think you're being flippant, see. But I reckon she's been dead maybe eighteen months, two years, that sort of time. And nobody is going to be able to remember a thing about it – not who was in the valley, or who came through, or anything. Police work is very difficult, Miss Quy. Nobody local has gone missing, that I do know; so we will be looking for a missing person in the whole of the bloody kingdom – all fifty million of them.'

'If you're right about the timescale,' Imogen told him, 'try matching your body against the missing persons register for May Swann.'

It took Imogen a little while to organise her return home. She couldn't drive her car; but Lady Buckmote, on being appealed to, joyfully rose to the occasion. She would drive to Shrewsbury, bringing her son, ('He might as well make himself useful now he's passed his test,') and Megan Evans would drive Imogen in her car as far as Shrewsbury, where she would be glad to go shopping. From Shrewsbury Megan would take the bus back up the valley, John Buckmote would drive Imogen's car back to Cambridge, and Imogen and Lady B. would motor home together in comfort. Lady Buckmote could not wait, she said, to hear how a respectable woman like Imogen contrived to be set upon by savage dogs in a remote part of Wales – and in term time, too!

Before leaving Quarry Farm, Imogen took her little camera from the glove box of her car, and got a couple of snapshots of the quilt. Then she and Megan set off for Shrewsbury. The journey started early, with diversion to make a farewell visit to Gwenny, just long enough for Imogen to be weighted down with a bag of scones, a jar of honey, a pot of home-made lemon curd, and fierce admonitions to come back sooner next time.

'Do you know just where they found that body?' Imogen asked Megan, as they drove out of the village.

'Up there – where the tarpaulin is pinned over the ground – do you see it?' Megan waved vaguely to her right, but didn't take her eyes off the road. 'It's right above the cottage.'

'Happy Chappy's?'

'That's it.'

'Megan, exactly what is Happy Chappy called?'

'His real name? I don't know, really. He's always called that. He's a miserable man – really stuck-up – never talks to anyone here, pulls a face if you give him good morning. And one of his friends called to him across the road, some name like 'happy' – 'cheery' or 'jolly' or something, and it sort of stuck. It's sarcastic, you would call it.'

'Did someone tell me he came from Cambridge?'

'I don't know,' said Megan cheerfully. 'From England somewhere, sure enough.'

19

As soon as they were back, Lady B. took Imogen immediately to Addenbrooke's to have her leg X-rayed, and safely plastered up. The casualty officer in Addenbrooke's expressed admiration for the skill with which his colleague in Wales had dealt with the fracture – and all without the benefit of X-ray, as Imogen told him.

'I believe he *is* good,' Imogen agreed. 'Good enough to treat a cow.'

'Oh, he mustn't do that,' said the casualty officer, looking alarmed. 'It isn't legal.'

'Well, of course,' said Imogen, wincing as he removed the splint, 'vets do train much longer than doctors.'

'Relatively simple organisms, people,' he said cheerfully.

'From the neck down, anyway,' she said.

'What? Oh, quite. Hold quite still now . . .'

Imogen's return home, garnished with fresh plaster, still warm, and assisted by Lady B., took on the shape of a great event – she opened the door to a rush from the breakfast room of Josh and Fran, colliding with each other in the hallway, and both talking at once.

'She's been back several days, Imogen, but I didn't know how to let you know . . .'

'Where have you been? *What have you done to yourself?* I've been so worried about you!'

'Since when,' said Imogen, smiling severely at Fran, 'has it been any business of a tenant to worry about a landlady?'

'I'll leave you then, m'dear. I see you're in safe hands,' said Lady B. 'William will be fretting.'

'Thank you,' said Imogen, squeezing Lady B.'s arm before releasing it, and transferring her weight to Fran's extended hand.

And Imogen's injury at least served to divert attention for the moment – it caused Fran and Josh to rush around making her comfortable and fixing a sandwich supper and a mug of chocolate, and gave her time to think carefully what she was going to tell Fran.

But for the moment Josh and Fran were too eager to tell her what had been happening to them to pay much attention to exactly how and where and why Imogen had broken a leg.

Fran had relented, it seemed, and phoned Josh almost as soon as Imogen had left in search of her. She had borrowed her father's car.

'I was a bit afraid of it at first, it's a socking great thing with lovely paint work—'

'Is it a Rover 3.5 coupé?' asked Imogen.

'Something like that. I don't know really what it is.'

'Giving the sex a bad name,' said Imogen, obscurely.

Fran ran on: 'Anyway, I trollied round tourist bits of Wales for a while, but it wasn't any good. Nobody could remember him, and the hotels don't keep their registers long enough. Actually I found two that had kept their '78 registers, and it took ages to go through them . . .'

'Fran, what made you think of Wales?'

'Melanie thought that's where it was.'

'Oh, of course.'

'You must be awfully tired, Imogen, what with that long journey, and then going to the bonesetter. We must let you sleep . . .'

But they were still standing there, looking at her expectantly.

'This thing is,' said Josh, 'that Fran didn't realise how upset I would be if she didn't phone. And I didn't realise how upset *she* would be . . . and when we realised we could see, really, that it must be because we were, well, a bit over-sensitive about each other, so we decided . . .'

'. . . to get engaged,' Fran finished for him.

'My dears, I'm so glad!' said Imogen. 'And truly amazed.'

'What's amazing about it?' asked Josh. 'Don't you think we suit each other?'

'You'll do beautifully,' said Imogen. 'I just didn't think people got engaged these days.'

'Well, they don't really. But the thing is,' Fran said, 'we can't get married very soon; we don't see how we can live together till we can afford a place, so we have come to an understanding. And that's an engagement in the language of your generation, isn't it?'

'In my generation,' said Imogen crisply, 'an engagement got announced in *The Times* and led to the purchase of a ring.'

Fran held out her right hand. It was adorned with a Christmas cracker ring, set with a big glass ruby. They all laughed.

'Do something for me, Josh,' said Imogen.

'Anything I can,' said Josh.

'Could you take my camera from the car, and get the film in it developed and printed urgently. I need big prints – seven by fives should do it. The film isn't finished, but you can make the camera rewind, and I don't mind junking the rest of the film.'

'I thought your car was in Wales,' said Josh.

'*WALES?*' said Fran. 'Oh, Imogen!'

'John Buckmote should have brought it back and parked it outside by now,' said Imogen, avoiding Fran's eye. 'I'm spaced out. I really must go to bed.'

'We'll talk in the morning,' said Fran. 'I can see it wouldn't be humane now.'

Josh, it turned out, presumably anxious not to upset his testy dear one just as things came clear between them, had not told Fran that he had confided in Imogen, or that Imogen had been concerned enough to go in search of her. Fran of course had not seen the photograph. Over breakfast Imogen explained how she had found it, how she had recognised the shape of the hill in the background, how she had driven off . . .

Fran studied the photograph carefully. The great Gideon; Melanie, slender, smiling, leaning against Gideon, and wearing a flowery frock; a farmer; the pale shape of a hill rising behind them.

'So off you went,' said Fran cheerfully. 'What did you find?'

'I'm afraid I might have found May Swann.'

'*May Swann?* What did she have to say for herself?'

'Nothing, I'm afraid. If it was May Swann . . . she was very dead.'

'Dead. And in Wales . . .'

'It becomes clearer by the minute, Fran dear, that we are stumbling around in something very dangerous. Of course the body may not be May Swann's . . . but—'

At that moment there was a cheerful rap on the back door, and Josh bounced in. He tossed on the kitchen table between them a packet of photos, with the logo of a one-hour print service on the envelope.

Imogen opened it while Josh bestowed a good-morning kiss on Fran, and spread the prints out on the table. Only a faint impression of the delicate and subtle beauty of the quilt had survived transformation to glossy photographs. But when Fran disengaged herself and sat down again Imogen had the gratification of seeing her face as she looked at the prints. She picked up the nearest one, and frowned at it.

'This is Gideon's maths,' she said. 'His famous pattern. Made into a quilt. It's beautiful; but how bizarre . . .'

'What perhaps you can't see from a small photo,' Imogen told her, 'is that it's an old quilt.'

'It can't be older than 1979,' said Fran.

'It's much older,' said Imogen. 'Made in the 1920s, I should think.'

'But . . . Imogen what are you saying? And where is this astonishing quilt?'

'It's on the spare bed in Quarry Farm, in the Tanat valley,' said Imogen. 'And I think it tells us very clearly where your Summerfield man spent the summer of '78, and why that is a secret worth killing for. And why a biographer just back from a trip to Wales may be in great danger.'

'We've got to call the police,' said Josh.

'You mean he stole his maths?' said Fran, bemused. She was holding a print in each hand, and staring at them. 'This is it, all right – an as-it-were Penrose tiling, but with ghostly heptagons, instead of pentagons . . . He didn't invent it at all; he lifted it! The rat! And golly, that does explain a sudden rush of brilliance to the head of a nondescript man, which stood to be explained, and which most people who knew him were baffled by! Imogen, this is dynamite! Wait till I tell Prof Maverack!'

A flash of affection accompanied Imogen's dismay. Trust Fran to consider only the impact on her project of a new discovery. A true seeker after truth! But how reckless!

'Fran you can't tell *anybody*! Certainly not Maverack, who was once in the Summerfield circle! Haven't you heard what I'm saying? Listen again . . .'

'Call the police,' said Josh.

'Janet Summerfield has been persecuting the people in that farmhouse, trying by every means fair or foul to acquire the quilt,' said Imogen. 'And it's only because it happens to be in a tight little enclave of Wales, where the English stick out a mile, and up an unmade track over private land, and in a farm with guard dogs that she hasn't managed it.'

'She can't get the quilt herself, so she's taken to killing anyone who comes close to finding out about it?'

'It certainly looks like it, doesn't it?'

'I'll call the police, if you won't,' said Josh. 'I'm not taking risks with Fran's safety.'

'We need to think. Will police enquiries make Fran any safer? I'm not sure.'

'She'll be safer if the mad woman is locked up.'

'What I feel like doing straight away,' said Imogen, 'is talking to my friend Mike Parsons, of the Cambridge police. Getting his advice. Will you hold your horses till I've done that, Josh?'

'I suppose.'

'And, Josh, I suddenly don't feel very safe in a house containing two women. You wouldn't like to move in with us for the moment, would you, and offer a little manly protection?'

She watched them exchange glances. Fran said, 'Imogen, I thought my rental agreement with you ruled out having anyone living in the flat, besides me?'

'I'm a free woman,' said Imogen happily. 'I can vary my terms.'

Shirl drove Imogen into work the next day. Work was possible, but biking to work was not. Although Imogen had sentimentally invited Josh under her roof she didn't want to live permanently under his eye. She could easily analyse the sentimentality; just because her own life hadn't dealt her winning cards in the love suit didn't mean she wasn't willing to speed love on its way for others. In fact she was probably more willing. Heaven keep her, she reflected, from the sourness of frustrated middle age!

Imogen had thought of something she could do. She could find a way to tell Janet Summerfield that Fran had found out where Gideon was in August '78. If the woman thought that Fran was convinced that he was at Tenby, say – she would perhaps relax, and then Fran would be safe for the moment. As long as she could refrain from telling anyone the fascinating truth for a little longer.

However the simplest way to convey misleading information to Janet Summerfield was to ring her up and tell it to her, and for that purpose Imogen proposed to use her office phone, so not getting overheard.

'Summerfield, J' was of course not in the Cambridge book – she lived at Castle Acre – but directory enquiries provided it. Imogen waited till the end of her office hours, when the last minor ailment had been dealt with. In fact, she reflected ruefully, being injured

139

herself was wonderful magic medicine – it made everyone cheer up at once, and make jokes. In fact, a fake plaster would be a handy thing to have around . . . When peace returned, and she had put up the 'closed – next clinic at—' sign on her door, she rang the enemy.

'Mrs Summerfield? I met you once, when you came to collect papers from my tenant, Miss Bullion – no, don't hang up, please, I have some news for you.'

Silence – but not a cleared line.

'Miss Bullion, as you perhaps know, was anxious to discover where your husband spent some weeks of 1978. She has found the answer, and will now be able to complete the biography in time for the publisher's deadline. I thought you might like to know that.'

'She has found . . . what has she found?' There was no mistaking the note of anxiety – even terror – in the voice.

'That he spent the time in a hotel in Tenby, that has miraculously kept its registers for the past fifty years.'

'*Tenby?* Is she quite sure?'

'Very. She seems exuberant.'

'As well she might be, succeeding where others have failed. Tell me, did she say he was alone – or was he with someone in this Tenby hotel?'

Imogen was taken by surprise by this question. She shouldn't have been.

'No; he seems to have been with someone.' She spoke on the spur of the moment.

'That will have been Melanie,' said Janet Summerfield. Suddenly her voice sounded desolate, bleak. 'Well – I'm glad the book will be finished with no more trouble. It was kind of you to put my mind at rest. Surprisingly kind – in the circumstances.'

'Don't mention it,' said Imogen, putting the phone down, and aware as she did so how ridiculous it is to say 'don't mention it' to someone who just has.

She stomped across to her kettle, and made herself a cup of coffee. She was feeling guilty at telling such whoppers, and told herself that it was perfectly ridiculous at one and the same time to suspect a woman of being a serial murderer, and have scruples about telling her lies.

20

'I think I'll talk to you off-duty,' said Mike. 'Can you come to supper tonight?'

'Certainly I could; but won't Barbara find this all boring?'

'She owes me,' said Mike, 'considering the amount of talk I put up with about college architecture.'

'College architecture?'

'She's doing a training course to be a local guide. You must have seen them, leading little bands of multiglot foreigners around, waving headscarves on walking sticks as rallying points.'

'I've seen them.'

'One can train to do it. Barbara has fluent Spanish, so she thought she might escort disorientated Dagos . . .'

'Sometimes I wonder why I like you, Michael Parsons. But I'd love to come to supper. Isn't it short notice for Barbara?'

'Good chance for her to practise. She's doing a cookery course too.'

'What energy – I'll look forward to talking to her about it.'

'It isn't surplus energy,' he said, 'it's revenge for the long hours I work.'

Barbara didn't mention Mike's working hours, however, but seemed very pleased to see Imogen. Barbara had made the little house very bright and cheerful; now it was all done she needed an occupation. The Cambridge Guide course was fascinating – she gave Imogen a thumbnail history of St Agatha's full of graphic detail. Did Imogen know that the college had nearly pulled down Old St Giles, and built a Victorian church in its stead? Did she know that the bumps in the linenfold panelling in the hall had been inflicted by Civil War soldiers, billeted in the college, who had used the hall to stable their horses? They had fixed rings for tethers to the panels . . . Imogen was more than willing to be told, and the food was delicious, though perhaps rather rich.

After supper, over coffee, she gave Mike an account of the journey into Wales.

'It was you, was it?' said Mike. 'I might have known!'

'What was me?'

'Setting PC Jones on to May Swann. He's found her.'

'So it was her?'

'He found a DB that matches her. A murder enquiry is in progress. Someone in records let me know because mine was the last enquiry after her. And, Imogen, I need hardly tell you that amateur detectives are unwelcome in murder enquiries. If they are on the wrong tack they are a fearful waste of police time; if they are on the right tack they are putting themselves in personal danger.'

'I am chiefly concerned in getting Fran out of personal danger.'

'But she has come home safe and sound. You have no real reason to think she is in danger, honestly, have you?'

'The danger seems to centre round that quilt.' Imogen was putting off telling Mike that she had rung Janet Summerfield with a cock-and-bull story about Tenby.

'Well, look at it our way,' said Mike. 'Found – one DB, on a remote patch of mountainside, head bashed in. Deceased known to have been carrying best part of two hundred and fifty pounds, empty purse found with body. No special need to explain presence of visitor in famous beauty spot overrun with tourists half the year. Theft is the obvious motive.'

'But . . .'

'*You* tell us that some five miles away from the interment of the victim, on the further side of the local town or village, is a farmhouse containing a quilt that you think might explain the crime via a tangled and extensive chain of guesswork . . . but May Swann probably didn't find the quilt at all. Your friends at Evans's farm didn't mention anyone except Janet Summerfield, now did they?'

'She didn't have to find the quilt to be in danger. She merely had to convince someone that she might be about to find it.'

'And then they would kill to stop her? They would kill to protect the reputation of a famous man against a recherché and far-fetched resemblance between an academic paper and a patchwork quilt?'

'Mike, there's too much coincidence here. Isn't it very strange that Summerfield's biographer should be found dead within a few miles of that quilt?'

'That sort of coincidence is like ley lines – look for it and you find it everywhere. People don't murder for these strange and curious motives, Imogen. Murder is very risky. People do it for down-to-earth, gutsy reasons, like money, lust, rage, jealousy.'

'Cambridge people might murder for what you call fancy reasons, Mike. Things of the mind matter a lot here. You can get thrown out of the University for stealing other people's work.'

'But murdered?'

'So you don't think that the mysterious fate of biographers is going to play much part in the enquiry into May Swann's death?'

'I think they will be looking for tramps and drop-outs who might have been in the valley at the material time . . .'

'Mike, what would it take to get you to take this seriously?' asked Imogen, desperately.

'A confession. We like confessions. As you know, we regularly beat them out of people . . .'

'I don't think you should say that even as a joke.'

'I suppose you're right,' he said, suddenly thoughtful. 'But the truth is most crimes are solved because someone confesses. Most confessions are made willingly enough; and most are not later revoked. Most motives are humdrum. A policeman's life is not a thrilling one . . .'

'What do you think I should do next?'

'My dear girl, I think you should do nothing. Nothing first, second or last. I can't believe your Fran's life is in danger from a serial murderer obsessed by biography. Stop worrying.'

'And what will you do?'

'Confidential. I *might* just make sure that someone digs out Professor Maverack's statement and draws it to the attention of the murder enquiry officers. Just as I might dig out the death certificate of your Mark Zephyr, and confirm that the cause of death is given as meningitis. But I can't say that I will.'

Imogen considered. She understood confidentiality. She needed to, in her job. There was no point in pressing him any further.

She steered the talk back to Barbara, and it rambled around the colleges, and arrived at the wrought iron gates at the entrance to Newnham College, which had once, Barbara said, been damaged in a riot.

'A *riot*? In Newnham?' Imogen was amazed. 'What was it about?'

'The undergraduates objected to women being given the titles for their degrees.'

'Oh – I think I remember something about that. You could sit for a degree, but you weren't allowed to call yourself a Cambridge BA?'

'That's it. I think. It's complicated. In 1920 Cambridge voted against admitting women. In 1921 they were admitted to "titular" degrees. They couldn't be full members of the University till 1948.'

'Heavens!' said Imogen.

'Among the other reasons given for the foot-dragging,' said Barbara gleefully, 'was a desire to be different from Oxford, which had let women in in 1919.'

'And there was a riot?'

'When the vote was taken in 1921. The undergraduates massed outside the Senate House while the votes were counted, chanting "We won't have women!" and then they surged off to Newnham and smashed up the gates with a stolen handcart. The Union offered to pay for the damage later. We are supposed to be able to point out to the tourists the signs of the repair to the iron work, but I admit I can't see it. Have a look yourself, next time you're passing, Imogen.'

'I will,' said Imogen. 'Golly. The past is a foreign country all right. I wonder what the undergraduates of 1921 would have said if they had foreseen mixed colleges and slot machines dispensing condoms?'

'They'd have said Hurrah if they had any sense,' said Mike.

'The women perhaps wouldn't have,' observed Barbara.

'My mother always hated the idea of mixed colleges,' said Imogen. 'But I just thought she was an old stick-in-the-mud. I wish I could talk to her about it now. She was at Girton; and it seems there was no love lost between Girton and Newnham . . .'

The conversation meandered along about the relative merits of co-ed colleges and schools until it was time for Imogen to go home.

Cambridge colleges are immortal. In the distant past some foundations were lost to the chances of time; recently, though a few have been born and nearly all have been metamorphosised in harmony with modern ideas like the equality of the sexes, none have died. None have died, and therefore none have paid death duties. The custodianship of their buildings, and their traditions, like the music in King's College and Trinity chapels, is a burden lovingly discharged. Colleges with canny bursars have prospered. St Agatha's was not among the very wealthy, has never had anyone like J.M. Keynes as bursar, and though it is not on the Backs, and has only a modest antiquity to its buildings, it feels, nowadays, the chill of the *Zeitgeist*. Once every five years, therefore, in the winter vacation, a judicious space after Christmas, it throws a splendid party for a group of its alumni; a concert is performed in the Wyndham Library, a feast is given in the hall, the Master makes a speech in which the underlying appeal for money is gracefully disguised in elegant rhetoric. The handsome Jacobean courts are available for returners to occupy – in their own old rooms as far as possible, while any money-making conferences the bursar may have rented rooms to are shunted off into the Waterhouse building on Chesterton Lane. Retired senior members are expected to turn out and recognise, or, at a pinch pretend to recognise, their sometime pupils, and a good time is had by all.

Quite often, in the course of the jollifications, or a little later, the college receives windfall gifts. A purchase of books for the library is sponsored; a bit of restoration and repair, which the Master has ruefully mentioned in his speech, and promised to undertake 'as soon as funds are available' is suddenly possible, with a donor's name discreetly inscribed nearby. A new scholarship is endowed – the possibilities are many. And the effect is not necessarily felt at once; many of the guests go home and alter their wills rather than handing out largesse immediately.

These gatherings require Imogen to man her office all day, and be on call at night, or sleep in the college for the duration. So many tottery old fellows on sticks, negotiating the undulant worn treads of the stairs to hall and chapel – drinking better port than they are used to, and therefore often more – losing their pills as they unpack in unfamiliar rooms – even falling in the river, or off bicycles imprudently borrowed, under the impression that riding a bike and propelling a punt are skills once learned never forgotten . . . There is nearly always a need for first aid, or worse, an ambulance. Imogen, who usually rarely recognises anyone who was up while she held her post, manages to enjoy it for all that. A plangent atmosphere of nostalgic joy prevails. On finding that their college still remembers them, the old boys, and latterly girls, are touched in both senses.

A short while after her return from Wales, Imogen, no longer in plaster, but still walking with a stick and aware of the irony, settled in to a student's room near her office for just such a weekend. There were rather fewer incidents than usual, and she decided she could afford to attend some of the events herself. The interesting one was a speech by Professor Maverack.

* * *

Maverack came up trumps, and delivered exactly the right sort of thing. He hoped that his eminent audience all kept diaries, even if they had not written memoirs. Of course he realised how difficult it had become to get such things published, even if they recounted eye-witness experiences of important historical events, but one never knew who might be the subject of biographical research, or indeed of biographies, in the future; in the age of the telephone the raw material for biography, and for history, come to that, was becoming very thin. He hoped none of them was so modest as to think they had no need to keep copies of their letters . . .

When he had finished, St Agatha's new librarian, a sharp and efficient Oxford graduate, stood up to say that the college library would be glad to receive gifts of manuscript memoirs and diaries, and, although careful archiving and cataloguing cost money, could promise to make them available for any future need. The lives and opinions of all members of college were of the greatest possible value to the college . . .

Thoroughly and subtly flattered the company dispersed towards lunch and a free afternoon.

Professor Maverack caught Imogen's eye as he left, with a little bevy of eager questioners around him. She was standing quietly at the doors, waiting for the last person to struggle up the stepped aisles in the tiered seating of the lecture hall, and get safely on level ground.

'That should do it?' he said quietly as he passed her.

'Oh, I should think so!' she said, laughing.

The slabs of roast meat, roast potatoes and vegetables glistening with butter that would be served up for lunch were too much for Imogen in the middle of the day. She slipped across the road for some filled rolls and a pastry, wrapped herself in her thick winter coat, and took them into the Fellows' Garden to chomp peacefully on a bench. The glory of the gardens crested in May; but Imogen liked the sight of the thickly populated herbaceous borders all tidy and labelled, and the snowdrops nearly ready to flower drifting between. The great weeping copper beech still held on to most of its rust brown leaves; and trees in lace are as pleasing as trees in leaf. She sat on a bench in a kind of outdoor alcove made of curving shrubbery, and tipped her face upwards into the pallid sun.

She had finished eating, and was thinking of going to her office to make herself a cup of tea, when a sound from beyond the bushes caught her attention. Audible between the bursts of birdsong was a human voice, quietly crying. Imogen got up and walked round the shrubbery, to find herself staring at Janet Summerfield, who was sitting weeping on a bench opposite hers.

'Can I help?' said Imogen. It was almost a conditioned reflex.

'No. Go away,' was the answer, and then, 'Who are you? Do I know you?'

'I am Imogen Quy. The college nurse here. If you are in any way unwell I can help you.'

'But you have helped me,' said Janet Summerfield. She stopped crying. 'You were kind to me. You told me that Miss Bullion would be able to finish her work; and that *was* kind when I had been – shall we say *abrupt*? with you. You must be a very nice person.'

'I try,' said Imogen, blushing slightly. 'Do you want me to make you a cup of tea, find you an aspirin, get a taxi to take you home?'

Mrs Summerfield shook her head.

'Do you want to tell me what is wrong?'

'Dr Maverack's talk upset me,' Janet Summerfield said. 'I don't think it is fair – do you, Miss Quy?'

'I don't quite see . . .'

'Holding out a hope that their stupid diaries will be snapped up eagerly, when I know too well that even Gideon can't get a biography – without – without lots of trouble. I shouldn't have come, but I thought some people might remember me, and it would be nice to pass the time of day with some of Giddy's – some of my late husband's friends.'

'Well, isn't it? Nice to meet old friends, I mean.'

'I haven't spotted anyone yet. Except Dr Bagadeuce. He seems very busy. I suppose they invite people from lots of different years . . .'

'Yes they do. I'm sorry there's nobody here you know. Would you prefer to go home?'

'That's it, I wouldn't. It's like the grave there. Quiet as death. Nobody to talk to from one week's end to the next. Never be a widow, Miss Quy – it's the loneliest thing on earth. You could go out of your mind wanting somebody to talk to.'

'Haven't you any friends?' Imogen asked her quietly. Imogen's professional demeanour was firmly in position.

'I've quarrelled with all the old ones. Not that there were many. I need to make new ones. Will you be my friend, Miss Quy?'

So, suddenly Imogen faced a moral choice. Easy to say yes – and make oneself into a betrayer by and by.

'No,' she said. 'I can't be your friend. Because, you see, I know why you did it.'

'You know?'

'So do others, now. I've told other people.' But though this sentence was supposed to deter Janet Summerfield from launching an instant attack, Imogen knew she wouldn't. She didn't feel in any danger at all.

'And you think it's dreadful? You think there isn't anything to be said for me at all?'

'Murder is dreadful,' said Imogen quietly. 'I do think so. Yes.'

'I tried to talk him out of it first,' said Janet. She was staring at Imogen wide-eyed, like a child trying to get out of trouble with a parent. 'He wouldn't listen. He didn't care about me at all. Can you imagine what that was like, Miss Quy?'

Imogen bit back the question burning on her tongue – *whom did you try to talk out of it?* and said instead, 'I'm not sure that I can; tell me.'

21

'I had a life of my own, once,' Janet Summerfield said. 'I had a good singing voice. I used to do concerts. Recitals – *lieder* – that sort of thing. I didn't know when I married him that Gideon would not be able to work with a single note of music audible from anywhere in the house – even someone humming while they worked in the kitchen, or singing scales at the bottom of the garden. I always thought mathematicians were musical – didn't you think they were?' She turned to Imogen a tear-stained face with an expression of mute appeal.

'I think many of them are,' said Imogen. 'What bad luck for you.'

'I couldn't practise enough, you see. I just had to give it up. I had to give everything up. Well, if you weigh in the balance a second-rate voice, against first-class mathematics . . .'

'But it doesn't really work like that, does it?' Imogen mused softly.

'It did for me. I really admired Gideon. He was much the cleverest person I had ever met; that's why I married him really. I admired him. He couldn't have wanted his work to succeed any more than I did. It was what I lived for. You do see?'

'The Dorothea Brooke syndrome?'

'Oh, but my Gideon's work was *real*. Not rubbish like Casaubon's. It was worth sacrificing oneself for.'

'You were the conventional old-fashioned wife, you mean, putting her husband first in every way . . .'

'Not conventional – that wouldn't have done for Gideon at all. He was a free spirit, Miss Quy. He *despised* convention. We all did.'

'All of you? You had a lot of friends?'

'We did once. Not latterly. Gideon didn't like visitors. They interrupted his work.' She fell silent.

'These friends,' Imogen prompted her. 'Melanie Bratch, for example?'

'Melanie wasn't my friend,' said Janet. 'She was Gideon's. He went off with her one summer, just to pay me out. I said the wrong thing, and he took umbrage and off he went with her. She was too young, you know, Miss Quy, to know what she was doing. I never blamed her. And I didn't mind him having a mistress. He was oversexed, you see. I couldn't keep up with him. I didn't mind; people sometimes wouldn't believe me, but I didn't. You expect creative people to be oversexed, don't you? Think how Picasso carried on with women! And my Gideon always came home. Always slept the night in his own bed. I didn't mind – not if it helped him work.'

'And you didn't mind if this got into the biography?'

'What? – Oh, no, I didn't mind that. Ian Goliard wouldn't have put it in, he said it was distasteful, the precious old twat! So I took the stuff about Melanie out of the files. But of course I thought any other biographer would find out and put it in. What has all this got to do with it? I was telling you about Gideon.'

Of course his biography has got to do with it! thought Imogen, but she kept quiet. A nasty feeling was engulfing her – like the shiver of fascination and revulsion that came over her in medical school when she was about to be asked to look at a lurid slide of injury or disease.

'I wanted children at first. Well, you do, when you get married – or you did in those days. But Gideon was afraid of the noise and the mess. He needed a regular life, with his meals nicely cooked and on time, and quiet and order in the house. So that was that really.'

'So for him you gave up music, and children, and latterly even friends?'

'Yes. I was always a support to him, Miss Quy, and happy to be, until . . .'

'He was a monster!' exclaimed Imogen. 'And yet you still want a flattering biography of him?'

'I want his work acknowledged. I want him to be famous as a great mathematician. Then at least it will have been worth it, all those years. Someone will say he owed a lot to a devoted wife!'

'They say he is about to be given the Waymark Prize. You would be happy at that – even though it is too late for him to enjoy it?'

'He didn't deserve to enjoy it!' She sounded suddenly ferocious. 'He would have wrecked it! He didn't give a damn about me! He just laughed when I told him how I felt about it—'

'I don't follow you, I'm afraid,' said Imogen. She was speaking softly.

'Let me put it plainly. The one sure thing about Gideon was his pride in his work. All those years he put it before everything else. Before me, certainly. Well, I understood that. To be honest, I wouldn't have amounted to much as a singer – it was easier to put my mind to helping Gideon than to pursue work of my own. I was disappointed at first; people treated him as just another don – not anything special by Cambridge standards. Then he published the new non-periodic pattern, and people woke up to his genius. I was really quite happy for a while; quite a few years. He liked it too. He got invited abroad to give lectures, and I went with him. And time went by, and people began to mention the Waymark Prize. And then he suddenly went dotty, and started to say he didn't deserve it and he was going to confess! Miss Quy, I *had* to stop him – you couldn't blame me, could you?'

'He was going to confess that he had cheated – that his great work was really someone else's?' asked Imogen. Once you actually looked at the awful sight directly, the feeling was different – neither revulsion, nor fascination, but a kind of cold, detached distress.

'I did everything I could think of! I implored him! Can you imagine the shame – the humiliation? I couldn't bear the disgrace. After everything I had done for him he was going to drag us in the mud, and he laughed. He said it was nothing to do with me. And it wasn't as if he had pinched work from a colleague – was it? It wasn't *mathematics* he took – just a pattern that some stupid old cow of a Welsh farmer's wife botched up! I kept telling him it took his genius to see what was special about the pattern anyway. But he wouldn't listen. So I had to kill him. Do you see?'

But Imogen was not sure what she saw. Just possibly total mania. 'How did you do it?' she asked.

'We – I – put stuff in his food. And I didn't care. I'd rather go to prison for murder than live through the disgrace!'

'It was so easy you weren't afraid to go on to kill others . . .'

'What do you mean?' cried Janet, springing up. 'What others? What are you talking about? There weren't any others!'

'I think there were at least two others,' said Imogen, standing her ground.

Janet Summerfield sat down again, and fixed an icy stare on Imogen.

'I'm sorry I talked to you,' she said. 'You aren't kind at all, you're a vicious sort of bitch. Now you listen to me. You can't prove anything I've just told you. Not a thing. There isn't any evidence. The hospital pathologist filled in the form, and we got permission for cremation . . . There isn't any proof of foul play. And I shall deny every word of this conversation. And if you repeat a word of it I'll have a libel lawyer on you in three seconds flat, and I'll strip you of every penny you possess. Understand?'

'I understand you all too well,' said Imogen, sadly.

Janet Summerfield got up and strode away across the immaculate lawns, her tent-shaped ample coat billowing in the chill breeze. Imogen sat watching her go, and wondering about that very curious change of pronoun.

'I got a confession for you, Mike. But it's for the wrong crime.' Imogen was standing in front of Mike's paper-laden desk in the police station. 'Oh and it was unwitnessed, and retracted at once. But perfectly genuine, I do believe.'

'Sit down,' said Mike. 'Tell me all about it.'

Imogen launched into a précis, as accurate as she could make it, of what Janet Summerfield had said.

'I take it this woman is bonkers?' said Mike when she had finished.

'Stark raving. Aren't murderers often?'

'Philosophical question that. Difficult one. Was the Yorkshire Ripper bonkers? Sane people don't go out at night looking for women to murder – ergo, the Ripper was mad. But mad people aren't responsible for their actions – ergo, the Ripper wasn't a murderer. What's the proof he was mad rather than evil? Well, he must have been because sane people don't go out at night looking for women to murder . . .'

'I see the problem,' said Imogen. 'Do you like philosophy, Mike? I'm surprised; I had you figured as a practical man.'

'It's rather acute and relevant to what you tell me this morning,' he said. 'When a mad person confesses to a murder, it is possible that they are really mad, and therefore not really a murderer – or that they are really a murderer and not really mad, or that they are so completely round the twist that they will for motives obscure to we normal folk confess to murders that they never committed, literally.'

'You mean, aside from the question whether such people are responsible for their actions is the prior question, did they actually perform the actions confessed to?'

'You got it. Well, what do you think?'

'If she did kill him I must admit I understand her reasons. The trouble with vicarious careers, vicarious glory, is that one's self-respect is at the mercy of the lead actor; and when the great Gideon got an attack of conscience he thought it was no business of his wife . . . whereas she had sacrificed every other desire in life to foster just the reputation he proposed to self-destruct.'

'She had a motive then. Marriage is one continuous stream of opportunity. What about a method? I think you've told me twice now that meningitis is an A1 rock-solid non-suspicious cause of death.'

'I did tell you that; but since we last spoke I've discovered something. There's a drug called DNOC; it kills rapidly in a high enough dose, with symptoms – euphoria followed by high fever and collapse – that are rather like those of meningitis.'

'And is this stuff for sale at Boots?'

'No, of course not. It's a garden chemical; but some years back it used to be prescribed as an aid to slimming . . .'

'Golly . . .'

'And Janet Summerfield is unrecognisable, Fran told me, in her photo album because her weight went up and down so dramatically.'

'So she might have been prescribed these things . . .'

'And she might have hoarded them.'

'That's an awful lot of mights, Imogen.'

'Well, I agree that it's bizarre, but patients often do hoard pills instead of taking them. Or throw away prescription forms instead of collecting the medication, even when it's free.'

'And we are talking about one very crazy lady, in whom hoarding lethal drugs would be merely a bagatelle beside the other mad things she has done . . .'

'I'll bet the maddest thing she ever did was marrying that man in the first place.'

'You're almost certainly right about that,' said Mike. He was rocking himself back in his chair, chewing a pencil, with an expression of deep thought on his face.

'And then, she said "we" and then corrected herself. And that's really *extremely* odd, Mike.'

'A mistake of one word in a great outpouring? Surely not. She's so used to regarding herself as just a suburb of her husband's life she's probably lost the use of the first personal pronoun.'

Imogen frowned. 'The distinction between singular and plural is deeply embedded, isn't it? Could one utter a sentence in the wrong number?'

'But she corrected herself at once, you say.'

'All the same . . .'

'Well, what "we" could there be? Do you mean she had an accomplice? Who else might have liked to murder Summerfield? Hang about – didn't you say he had a mistress?'

'Yes, he did; but I don't see . . .'

'Well, neither do I, I must admit. And I'm really not supposed to go on fishing expeditions. Of course, in view of what you tell me I could go and interview Janet Summerfield—'

'Nothing stops *me* from going on fishing expeditions,' said Imogen. 'The mistress's name is Melanie Bratch . . .'

'You know, murder enquiries are intrinsically dangerous, Imogen. And you live alone in the vacation, or with only your precious Fran in the house.'

'We have just acquired Josh as a bodyguard,' Imogen told him. 'And I will be careful.'

'Well then, since this is not yet an official enquiry, why don't you talk to the mistress before I talk to the wife? See if you can find out anything. And let me know immediately you have done it. OK?'

It was, of course, more than flesh and blood could bear not to tell any or all of this latest development to Fran. Fran's reaction startled Imogen, who had been thinking of it as a dismally sad story. But Fran was ecstatic.

'Corrumbers, Imogen! If we could prove *that*! And if any of that is true – think of the story line! Our hero in a moment of weakness steals his theme – enjoys the glory for many years, and then when he is about to gain the ultimate crown repents – suddenly conscience driven, he is ruthlessly silenced. Wow! What a book I will be writing! The first biography of a scholar to combine detection and moral drama! I'll be famous!'

'That'll be all right, then,' said Imogen drily. She had instinctively been seeing matters through Janet Summerfield's eyes – the wife's tale – but Fran of course, as was quite proper in a biographer, had seen Gideon as the central protagonist. Interesting, thought Imogen – do I always tend to see the world through women's eyes? More, even, than the fiercely egalitarian Fran? Well, after all, you wouldn't expect a young person nowadays to have much sympathy for the Dorothea syndrome.

'Fran, what do you think about that I/we business? Do you think someone who was acting alone might have said "We . . ."?'

'Hmm,' said Fran. 'I don't think I would. So you mean somebody else was involved?'

'If so, who? Who else had a motive? Melanie?'

'I don't see what her motive was. *She* wasn't going to bathe in reflected glory, surely? And, Imogen, she's nice. She just wouldn't have. If you talked to her you'd see.'

'I shall be talking to her. Do you want to come?'

Fran considered. She leant back in the battered armchair by Imogen's fire, and thought about it for some time.

'In one way, I'd love to,' she said. 'But if you want confidences, two are better than three, aren't they? You have a talent for being confided in, Imogen, and I think I'm rather too bright and bouncy for it. You'd better go alone. But I want a playback of every syllable she says – right?'

22

Melanie readily agreed to see Imogen. But on opening the door to her, said, 'I'm not sure I can help, Miss Quy. I told that nice young woman Frances Bullion everything I could about Gideon. But I don't mind talking to you, of course. It's nice to have a visitor. I'm very lonely since Gideon died.'

Melanie took Imogen's coat, and gestured her to sit down. A little tray sat ready on a coffee table, with biscuits and two glasses of sherry. Melanie was moving around slowly, on two sticks, her need for sheltered housing very apparent, but she seemed mentally quite alert and capable. Imogen studied Melanie – in whom the beauty she had once had was still, if not quite visible, deducible. The flat was neat, and rather crowded – Melanie had brought more things than the planners had considered necessary for sheltered old ladies.

'It isn't Gideon I want to ask about,' Imogen began. 'It's Janet. I need your advice, and this conversation might upset you.'

'Why might it? I don't know very much – or care very much – about Janet. She made the man I loved miserable for many years.'

'I have a problem, you see. She has been behaving in a rather crazy sort of way . . .'

'That's nothing new.'

'But it leaves me in a dilemma how to react to something she told me.'

'What did she tell you?'

'That she – and some other person not named – had killed her husband by putting something in his food.'

Imogen was watching Melanie closely as she said this, but she saw no expression of terror on the other woman's face.

'She's really gone off her trolley, then,' said Melanie. 'She made a lifetime's occupation of being the great man's wife; why would she put herself out of a job?'

'Because he was about to own up to having pinched his theorem from somewhere, and she couldn't stand the disgrace.'

Melanie suddenly looked rather grey. 'Janet certainly would have hated that,' she said. 'Enough to kill for? Possibly. Oh, poor, poor old Giddy! I can't bear to think about it!' She covered her face with both hands, and began to weep quietly.

And so it was evident to Imogen that Melanie believed this story at once.

In a little while she recovered her composure. 'I suppose she told you she had sacrificed everything to his need to do great work?'

'Yes, she did. He certainly sounded very selfish, in her account. As though his work had cost her dear. Isn't that right?'

'It's the wrong way round. From the moment he married her she drove and hounded him. She shooed away his friends, and shut him into silent rooms, and organised every moment of the day for him to work in it. She wouldn't even let him out for lunch, sometimes. He had to have sandwiches and a thermos of coffee at his desk so that he didn't have to stop. Even on holiday he had to sit there with paper and pencil part of every day, in case he got inspired. It absolutely quenched him. His sort of work came freely or not at all – he couldn't force it. And she let him know in no uncertain terms that she wasn't doing all that just for an average sort of Cambridge man – she wanted glory. Poor Giddy couldn't live up to her. He used to come to me for a bit of peace.'

'But she had made large sacrifices for him?'

'Twaddle. The first time she got a bad review for a recital she gave it all up and blamed him. He would have liked children; she said the noise would stop him working . . . Heavens! I've suddenly realised what he would have been going to confess – he was going to say he got his pattern from some quilt – right?'

'Yes. Did you know about that?'

'Not really. But I remember when we ran off together that summer long ago, there was a quilt in the farm where we stayed that he was awfully struck by. It rained a lot, and he copied the pattern in his notebook – every piece, right to the borders.'

'Did he ever tell you he had based his discovery on it? Or that he was going to confess?'

'No. But then the one thing in heaven and earth we never mentioned to each other was his sanctified work.'

'And I can take it that the other person who might have been involved in killing the poor man was not you?'

'No it was not. I would have died myself sooner than harm Giddy, whatever he had been up to.'

'Do you have any idea who it might have been?'

'No. I know who his friends were – apart from college friends of course. Ian; but he was abroad a lot. Leo – he went to America. He's back now, of course, and I see him now and then, but he didn't get back till after Gideon's death. Meredith – the trouble is I can't think what motive any of them would have. We were just a group of friends; rather jolly friends in our youth. And then life separated us and scattered us, the way it does. When we were young we were all hungry to achieve something, to get famous – and most of us managed some contribution. Most of us got realistic, and more modest year by year. It was only Janet who was implacable. I didn't give a damn about Gideon's maths – I would have hated it if he had become any more famous, I saw less of him when he was glorying around on lecture trips. I just liked him, for himself. He could have given up maths and taken up knitting for all I would have cared.'

'And you don't know anything about these successive biographers?' Imogen asked.

'I know Ian got very fed up with it. He came to see me before he went back to Italy. Mind you, a biography written by Ian would have been – well – mannered. Oblique. Mostly about Ian.'

'He's in Italy? Are you sure he's all right?'

'I got a postcard only last week. It's on the mantelpiece. You can look if you like.'

The card showed the view of Florence from the Piazzale Michelangelo. The message read: 'Traffic awful. Crowds awful. Glad you're not here. Ian.' It was postmarked five days ago.

'I'm not much help, am I?' said Melanie, smiling ruefully up at Imogen. There was a glint of tears in her eyes. 'What will happen to Janet? Will they get her for it?'

'They'll try,' said Imogen. 'I rather hope they succeed.'

'You know, the only clever thing *I* ever did,' said Melanie, showing Imogen to the door, 'was busting in on Janet's circle of satellite young men and carrying off Gideon for three days . . .'

Medical diagnosis is an arcane mixture of hunch and logic. When Imogen was training as a doctor – a training she had thrown over to go to America with her fiancé – diagnosis had been what most fascinated her about her studies. A crime, like a disease, throws up symptoms all over the place, and the needful art is to see the pattern. Patterns in these matters are like Pascal's wheelbarrow – *c'est infiniment simple, mais il fallait y penser* – it's infinitely simple, but someone had to think of it – clear only with hindsight.

Sitting comfortably in her quiet, sunny sitting-room, Imogen set herself to the game of hunt-the-pattern. And part of the pattern is obvious enough. Having harried Mark Zephyr as she had been harrying Fran, Janet suddenly invites him to dinner and is kind and helpful. Whereupon Mark contracts meningitis, and dies. Just as Gideon himself had crossed swords with his wife, caught meningitis, and died. Could these deaths have been unrelated? Surely not. But there is a problem. For Janet has emphatically denied knowing anything about Mark Zephyr's death; and the only evidence against her on her husband's death is her confession made to Imogen. So why would she own up to one and hotly deny the other? I am missing something, thought Imogen.

Well, one possible reason, however unlikely, is that she did commit one murder, and she didn't commit the others. Think it through . . . Mark had dinner with Janet . . .

Imogen got up and went to the telephone. She dialled Pamela Zephyr's number. 'Pamela . . . Yes, I'd love another walk soon. Next fine weekend . . . Look, can you tell me something? That last evening, when Mark had supper with Janet Summerfield, was there anyone else there?'

'Yes, there was, now you come to ask. Some woman doctor with a funny name.'

'You can't remember the name? It might be important.'

'No . . . I don't think I can . . . It was very odd sounding; one of those names like Vivian, or Evelyn, or Hilary . . . Sorry, my mind's gone completely blank.'

'Well, would you let me know if it floats out of your subconscious any time? See you soon.'

Imogen put the phone down, and moved back to her sitting-room. She wasted a whole valuable hour, sitting thinking in her armchair, turning things over and over in her mind. It was nearly seven when she got up and went through to her kitchen to fix herself some supper. She saw the answerphone blinking as she went through the hall, and stopped to play her messages. The window-cleaner announced himself for tomorrow; Shirl wanted to know if Imogen would drive her to a quilt display at Hemingford Grey, in Lucy Boston's house.

'Lucy Boston made some of the loveliest quilts ever!' Shirl said. 'And you can see round the house and garden and be shown the quilts if you just look up P.S. Boston in the phone book, and call ahead to say you're coming! Shall we go soon?' Then call box blips, and Fran's voice. Fran said she wouldn't be in for supper. She sounded pleased.

'Dr Bagadeuce has asked me to have dinner with him in his rooms. He says he has something really good to tell me about Summerfield. Byee!'

Imogen put the phone down and went into the kitchen. She looked abstractedly into her fridge, having forgotten what she was doing, her mind on other things. There is a certain level of formality in college life that has become unusual in the world outside. Imogen thought of the Maths Fellow as Dr Bagadeuce, and addressed him, when she had any occasion to, as Dr Bagadeuce. But he was not a medical doctor, and she did know his first name. Dr Bagadeuce had one of those funny names like Hilary or Vivian – a name that could be that of a man or of a woman. Dr Bagadeuce was called Meredith . . . Imogen could almost hear the clicks as everything fell into place.

She ran back to the phone and dialled Mike's number.

23

For once Mike wasn't dismissive. He was galvanised at once. 'Get there. We're on our way,' he said. And the police were there before Imogen, though she ran out of the house at once and drove herself hell for leather into college. There were police cars parked at the college gate, blue lights flashing. Mike was in the porter's lodge, wearing jeans and a sweater.

'There's no way out of his rooms except down the staircase into the Fountain Court, it seems,' said Mike. 'We've got the college gates staked out. But we have to get there without being seen, and his windows overlook the court . . .'

Hughes, the senior porter, was visibly distressed. 'It would be much better if you let me telephone through to Dr Bagadeuce and tell him you are coming . . .' he was saying, his face a picture of misery.

'No!' said Mike sharply. 'French!' – he gestured to one of his uniformed colleagues – 'Stand here and make sure that *nobody* uses a phone!' To Imogen he said, 'It would only take a split second to flush food down the toilet, if we alarm him.'

'It won't worry him to see me walking across there,' said Imogen. 'My office is just beyond his staircase. And I could have anybody with me if they're in plain clothes.'

'Off we go then,' said Mike.

In fact Imogen's usefulness as a cover for Mike was limited, because he set off straight across the college lawns, instead of using the paths round the edges of the court, which she never did. But Dr Bagadeuce did not happen to glance out of his window. His rooms were on the ground floor. His 'oak' – the solid outer door closed when the inmates wanted privacy – was shut. Mike hammered imperiously upon it. And then, meeting no response, hammered again.

'Be patient, can't you – I'm just coming . . .' said a voice from within, accompanying the sound of keys being turned. 'What is it?' said Dr Bagadeuce, opening both outer and inner door. 'I'm otherwise engaged . . .'

Mike roughly shouldered him aside, saying 'Police', and disappeared within.

Dr Bagadeuce took a step towards Imogen, as though he was perhaps thinking of leaving, rather than returning to his room. The sight of two uniformed policemen standing behind her changed his mind. 'The invaluable Miss Quy,' he said, drily, seeing her. 'Well, you had better come in. I might perhaps need a witness.'

Imogen followed him in. Fran sat facing her across a table laid for dinner. The table was set behind the ample settee which faced the fire. It was covered with white damask, and laid with college porcelain and silver. Mike was standing beside it.

'Don't move, or touch anything, Miss Bullion,' he said to Fran. 'Just tell me who is eating what here.'

And Imogen saw that there were as many as six separate serving dishes on the table – three at each end.

'I don't understand . . .' said Fran. 'What is this?'

'Just answer the question,' Mike told her, sharply.

'He is a vegetarian, so he has made a separate meal for me . . .'

Dr Bagadeuce stepped forward, moving from behind Imogen with swift steps. 'It will be getting cold,' he said, taking one of the dishes up from the table. 'I'll put it to keep warm . . .'

'No you don't,' said Mike, grabbing the dish. 'I'm sending it to be analysed.'

'Ah,' said Dr Bagadeuce, and he sat down on his settee. He had turned very white.

'No doubt you can tell us what we shall find,' said Mike, coldly. 'Miss Bullion, have you eaten any of this – what is it? – stew?'

'No,' she said. 'We were just about to start . . .'

'Thank God,' said Imogen.

'I think,' said Fran to Dr Bagadeuce, 'that the implication of all this is that my friends believe you were about to poison me. Were you about to poison me?'

'Yes, Miss Bullion,' he said quietly. 'I was. I was determined to avert a disaster to my college.'

'And you think it is not a disaster to the college if a senior member murders a graduate student?' she said, incredulously.

'I did not expect to be found out,' he said. 'But you are right; I have brought about a worse calamity. I suppose I have no chance of persuading you, when you see what sacrifices I am prepared to make for St Agatha's, that you should not publish your discoveries about my late colleague?'

'But I appear to *be* the sacrifice,' said Fran.

'You might like to tell us what, on analysis, will be found in Miss Bullion's portion of that stew?' said Mike.

'I would not like. Why should I help you?' he said.

'It will be contaminated with DNOC,' said Imogen.

'You pestiferous meddling person,' he said, snarling at her. 'One might expect a college servant to put the college first!'

'Come, Dr Bagadeuce,' said Mike. 'Time to go.'

'Do you have to march me across the court in full view, like a common criminal?' Dr Bagadeuce said.

'You are a common criminal,' said Mike. 'But no; if you prefer we can leave via the gate on Chesterton Lane. We have police cars at every gate.'

'I want her with me,' said Dr Bagadeuce, gesturing at Imogen. 'I want a witness to ensure my safety.'

'I will see you off college premises, Dr Bagadeuce,' she said. 'And the moment you are driven away I will telephone your lawyer. I'll see you at home, Fran.'

A little group of them, therefore, walked across the second and third of the college courts, avoiding the main gate, going towards the back gate. Their route led them under the colonnade by which the chapel was approached, and past the large marble slab in the wall on which the names of college members who lost their lives in two world wars were inscribed.

Beneath this memorial Dr Bagadeuce halted. 'Look at this,' he said. 'Look how many lives were given from this one small college for the defence of England. No doubt for all these young men their college was an important part of the England they died to defend. If I was ready to kill, Miss Quy, I too would have killed for my college. But who will understand, let alone memorialise me?'

'Not I, I am afraid,' she said.

'Don't give me that!' said Mike, furiously. 'You are not just *ready* to kill, you have killed two people already. The victim we have just rescued would have been at least your third, perhaps your fourth.'

Dr Bagadeuce turned on him, snarling. 'You can't prove that! And you'd better be careful of saying what you can't prove! I shall deny everything you can't prove!'

'I shall prove enough,' said Mike. 'More than enough, trust me for it.'

24

You might think that narrowly escaping being poisoned would put you off your food, for a day or two. But Fran had had no supper, and declared herself ravenous. So Imogen took her out to supper at the Red Lion in Grantchester. They were just easing the car out of its parking space outside Imogen's house – parking was very tight these days – when they realised that the car lurking behind them ready to nip into the vacated slot, was Mike Parsons in a patrol car. Mike was very ready to be invited to join them, so they all piled into 'Rosy', Imogen's ancient little Nova, and tootled off to Grantchester. They settled down at a corner table to eat and talk.

'My saviour!' said Fran to Imogen tucking into game pie and chips. 'What would it have done to me?'

'What would what have done to you?'

'Dinner with Dr Bagadeuce.'

'It would have made you feel on cloud nine at first. Then over-excited, and feverish. Then brought on a very high fever, and with it convulsions, coma and death. It would have looked very like meningitis.'

'So he might have got away with it?'

'Perhaps not, this time. He was pushing his luck, going on doing it.'

'What I want from you,' said Fran, looking hopefully at Mike, 'is a blow-by-blow account of how you worked all this out.'

'Not me,' said Mike cheerfully. 'All down to Imogen.'

'Imogen then. Tell me all.'

'Well, to start with we both suspected Janet Summerfield of murdering biographers. She seemed so steamed up about everything. The mystery was her motive. After all, she it was who wanted the biography.'

'But she didn't want anything about that crucial summer . . .' said Fran eagerly.

'. . . because investigating that might lead someone to the quilt; she was terrified that the great Gideon would be unmasked as a cheat.'

'Why didn't she just get rid of the quilt?' asked Mike. 'She was ruthless enough.'

'As I know to my cost the approach to the quilt was guarded by fierce dogs. The owners were hostile. She tried all she could think of, but in vain.'

'So she hoped just to contrive to get a biographer who would let it rest, and use just what she wanted used. I see,' said Fran.

'Well, so, the moment I clapped eyes on the quilt – no, I tell a lie, I was a bit foggy at first – but little by little as I looked at the quilt I perceived that it was older than Summerfield's discovery, and that it provided the missing motive. So then I thought about method. Fran – do you remember telling me that you had embarrassingly failed to recognise Janet Summerfield in her family photographs because she kept losing weight and putting it on again?'

'Yes, – she certainly did,' said Fran.

'Well, I happened to be browsing in my medical dictionary the other day when my eye fell on DNOC. It used to be prescribed, long ago, as a slimming drug. So there I seemed to have it – motive, opportunity and method for Janet Summerfield to have killed Mark Zephyr. And then I found myself talking to her at the college party. So I said, "I know why you did it," and she suddenly poured out her heart to me and confessed – to having murdered her husband.'

'Right murderer – wrong crime!' said Fran.

'Exactly. So I prompted her about the others, and she hotly denied any knowledge. So hotly that I began to wonder if in fact there could have been someone else. Now, what does the name Meredith conjure up, Fran?'

'Some elderly female of posh extraction?'

'But it's also a man's name. It's Dr Bagadeuce's first name.'

'So the "Merry" they were all talking about in those jolly holidays they took . . .?'

'Could have been – was – him. And the Cambridge doctor near whose cottage in Wales poor May Swann was disinterred, the English man they called "Happy Chappy" because of his silly name, was likewise him.'

'But the motive and method applied only to Janet,' said Fran.

'His motive was related to hers. And do you know, he actually told me what it was, only I wasn't listening.'

'He told you?' said Mike.

'It was some time back, and about something else. He carried on rather madly about the honour of the college.'

'I don't get this bit at all,' said Mike.

'Well, it is fairly mad, I admit,' said Imogen. 'But it certainly doesn't do the college's reputation any good if one of its senior members is exposed as a plagiarist. And there are people – Dr Bagadeuce is one – who spend their entire lives devotedly serving the college, achieving nothing in the eyes of the outside world, but only their precious place here, in Cambridge . . .' She looked at her companions' expressions. They were both staring at her, looking unconvinced. 'Well, all right, he's plain crazy. But, Mike, I don't see how you can be a policeman in Cambridge, while not understanding a Cambridge sort of motive for crime.'

'Let me disillusion you, lady,' said Mike cheerfully. 'A diminishingly small proportion of crimes in Cambridge are committed by senior member of colleges.'

'Correction,' said Fran, winking at Imogen. 'A diminishingly small proportion of *discovered* crime in Cambridge is attributable to college fellows.'

'Mock away,' said Mike. 'But if you're not careful, I shall remember my official responsibilities, and not tell you what either of them said when questioned.'

'Oh, Mike!' Fran and Imogen both protested in unison.

'Well, since I have two lovely ladies hanging on my every word . . .'

'Is he always like this?' Fran demanded.

'Only when about to get a lot of credit for clearing up a murder or two,' said Imogen crisply.

'I deserve a lot of credit for listening to your paranoid suspicions,' said Mike. 'Even if it is later apparent that they were justified. Now do you want to hear about this or not?'

'Of course we do,' said Fran. 'Be quiet, Imogen.'

'Well, Janet won't repeat her admission to you, Imogen, that she dosed Summerfield's dinner. She says that Dr Bagadeuce had the run of her house, was an old and trusted friend, and could easily have stolen the slimming pills from her bathroom cupboard. She says she hoarded multiple packets of the stuff, and that at some time, she doesn't know when, it disappeared. She says she thought one of the cleaning agency's charwomen must have taken them. She says there is a black market for them since doctors stopped prescribing them.

Someone who nicked them could have sold them. She absolutely denies that her husband was going to confess to cheating.'

'Can she get away with this?' asked Fran.

'Probably not, in view of what Dr Bagadeuce says. He denied everything at first, until we told him that samples of the assailant's blood had been recovered from May Swann's clothing, and could be DNA profiled, and compared with his. Then he confessed.'

'I hope that was true, Mike,' said Imogen.

'The confession? You can bet it was.'

'The statement that the blood sample could be matched.'

'As true as I'm sitting here,' said Mike. 'What do you take us for? I used to think you read too many detective stories; now I think you read too many newspapers.'

'Sorry, sorry . . .'

'According to our dear Merry Bagadeuce, Janet Summerfield appealed to him for help in talking Gideon out of a public breast-beating. He appealed to Gideon's self-respect, and his loyalty to the college, and Gideon wouldn't listen. Gideon said his self-respect demanded that he owned up and gave credit where it was due. "Imagine giving credit for abstruse mathematics to some silly old biddy doing needlework!" Bagadeuce said. Having failed to talk the man out of it, he and Janet together decided to kill him. She handed over the DNOC tablets, and he cooked up a delectable meal with them . . .'

'*That's* why she said "we" killed him . . .' said Imogen.

'Yes. Must be. Well, then he gets incandescent with rage over her stupidity. Fancy commissioning a biography in those circumstances! Stupid cow, he calls her, thinking she could suppress awkward questions, and the biographer wouldn't ever find out about the quilt. But of course, there was now a lot to lose. Who would want to murder an old friend to keep something dark, and then have it come out and get published abroad anyway? Seeing off Ian Goliard was no trouble, he tells us. The man had various things in his own life that were best kept dark; he just succumbed to pressure and went abroad. But Mark Zephyr couldn't be shaken off. And there was plenty of DNOC left.'

'But was that both of them, or just him?' asked Imogen.

'Depends whom you believe. *He* says she invited Zephyr to dinner, in the full knowledge of what he, Bagadeuce, was cooking up in the kitchen; *she* says she doesn't know what we are talking about.'

'What about May Swann?'

'Well, he says they became frantically anxious that the quilt might give Gideon away; Janet went and stayed in his cottage and tried repeatedly to get it, and failed. Then May Swann, all innocent, telephoned Janet and told her that she had found some indication that Gideon had spent time in the Tanat valley, and was off to look for confirmation; and so Bagadeuce went at once to his cottage, and waited for her to turn up. He met her "accidentally" in the pub, bought her a drink, and lured her on to his land, by telling her that he thought his was the cottage Gideon had stayed in, and then he clunked her on the head with a flat-iron he kept for decoration on the stove, and buried her on the hillside above his garden.'

'And then I came along and began to ask questions about the same thing,' said Fran, looking queasy.

'Dr Bagadeuce kept trying to persuade Janet to quash the biography; but she had got crazy for the glory of that whatsit prize, and she was sure the biography would say what a noble wife the fellow had, so she wouldn't. And, young Fran, it's just as well you have a caring landlady, or you might be six feet deep by now.'

'What will happen to them now?' asked Fran.

'Remand in custody. At the trial, I don't know. A couple of good defence lawyers will make hay over the sheer ramshackle nature of the reasoning. She might get off, even. He won't if that DNA test sticks, as I think it will.'

'Aren't confessions enough?' asked Fran.

'Well, she hasn't confessed, except to Imogen. You'll have to testify, Imogen.'

'Oh, Lord,' said Imogen gloomily.

25

Over the next few days, with St Agatha's buzzing with gossip, Imogen found herself explaining her trains of reasoning, and the accompanying trains of event, over and over again to various listeners. It is a sad commentary on human nature that people who profess themselves horrified and appalled by some calamity, speak with shining eyes, and eager expressions, so that if you could not hear their words, but only watch them, you would suppose they must be delighted.

So the members of St Agatha's, all trying to be appropriately dismayed, displayed the usual *schadenfreude*. There were many senior members who had smarted in the past under some pompous rebuke from Dr Bagadeuce on the subject of their loyalty to the college. People who had been sniped at for baby-sitting their children, or being absent when a college meeting was in progress. Junior members who in general could not help rejoicing when a senior member trod on a banana skin – and what a banana skin being arrested for murder was!

The feverish atmosphere was deplorable, no doubt, but understandable. Imogen told her story to her colleagues. She forgot to tell them that she was visiting Dr Bagadeuce in prison, and bringing him his letters, and such treats as remand prisoners are allowed. She was not quite the only person to maintain horror in parallel with kindness; Lady Buckmote had also been visiting.

Fran, meanwhile, had become famous in the courts of St Agatha's; courted and questioned, and celebrated and invited to dinner. She complained to Imogen that the fuss threatened to slow down her delivery of the Summerfield biography. Leo Maverack was over the moon, and he invited Fran and Imogen for a 'tête-à-tête feast' in his rooms the following week. To Imogen's surprise and pleasure, Holly Portland was there, making up the fourth in the party. Holly could, and emphatically did, confirm that any quilt made in the twentieth century would be very closely datable.

'What a story it is!' Fran said happily, and not for the first time. 'Poor mediocre chap driven to overperform; tempted to steal his discovery; struck with late-onset remorse – losing his life as a consequence . . .'

'It is truly a brilliant story, said Leo Maverack benignly, giving Fran a smile of fatherly smugness. 'I wish I hadn't given it to you. I wouldn't have if I had had any idea that dull old Gideon would prove so fascinating. Oh, don't worry!' he added, seeing Fran's expression. 'I wouldn't dream of getting it back from you now. Indeed, just the opposite. I understand that Recktype and Diss will be glad to publish under your name, and with only a brief introduction from me. Your career as a biographer has started very well.'

'But . . .' said Fran, flushing with pleasure, 'How very kind of you, but I thought they needed your name to make publication of it possible.'

'So they did, when they thought the great Gideon had lived a blameless, and therefore boring, life. Now it turns into a morality play and climaxes with a murder or two, they think they could sell it with a dog's name on it, and yours will do very well. I did suggest you might write an afterword about the death and hard times of the biographers . . . or will you be too proud and scholarly to do that?'

'Not at all,' said Fran, 'it's part of the story. But, Dr Maverack, don't you get anything out of the project at all?'

'Oh, don't worry about me, m'dear!' he said, gleefully. 'I told you originally that I was too busy to write it myself? Well, so I was; I am writing a book of my own on the theory of biography. Its main thesis is the need to deconstruct the self-flattering falsehoods behind which people shelter, and which biographers often collude with. Your biography of Summerfield is going to give me just the most perfect example possible in support of my thesis. I am going to puff your book extensively in the course of mine, and we are both going to benefit.'

'Would somebody mind very much,' said Holly, 'telling me whatever it is you are all talking about?'

Eagerly they set about telling their stories all over again.

At the end of the evening Imogen asked Fran to ride her bike home, while she got a taxi. Her leg, healed but still unreliable, was aching. Holly at once offered Imogen a lift. Leo Maverack escorted everyone to the college gates, seeming reluctant to let them go.

'It's a fascinating thing about that quilt,' said Holly as they waited at the traffic lights at the end of Sidgewick Avenue. 'A really *new* quilt pattern – not just a variation in the placing of light and dark fabrics – is most unusual. So many millions of quilts have been made, by so many people, over so many years, that just about every possibility has been done before. Your Welsh farmer's wife must have been a genius in her way.'

At Imogen's front door they said good night.

'Oh, Holly,' said Imogen, 'I'd love to have you to dinner to meet some of my quilt-making friends. How long will you be around? When are you going back to the States?'

'I'm not going back, after all,' said Holly. 'I've been offered a research fellowship in textile history, right here in Cambridge. Dinner with you any time. Oh, and Imogen – watch out for that old fraud Leo Maverack – I'm sure he fancies you!' And she drove off before Imogen had time to congratulate her.

Imogen let herself into the house, and put some hot milk on the stove for chocolate – enough for Fran too. She took two paracetamol to quiet the aching in her healing leg. Funny that – Holly apparently used the word 'fraud' as a term of affection. For everyone else in Cambridge it was a term of abuse – serious abuse.

The paracetamol did not help her sleep. She lay awake, thinking. About the possibility that paracetamol makes you think. About the dreadful disgrace of cheating – gets you thrown out of Cambridge. About the miserable steal of taking your maths from someone's quilt . . . about Janet Summerfield and Dr Bagadeuce's shared contempt for 'some old biddy doing needlework . . .' It really wasn't as though their precious Gideon had stolen from a colleague. Not in their eyes. And yet Holly thought the quilt-maker must have been a genius.

And it was a few days later before the final penny dropped. Imogen was walking on the Roman road by the Gog Magog hills, on a lovely sunny and crisp late spring day. Her companions were Lady Buckmote, and Pamela Zephyr. They were there for the exercise, and each other's quiet companionship, and the conversation was intermittent and largely about the scurrying behaviour of the dogs, and the identification of various songbirds serenading them as they passed.

Imogen told Lady Buckmote that what with Professor Maverack's book, and Fran's book, the college could expect a little glory to make up for the disgrace of Dr Bagadeuce's homicidal devotion had cast upon it. Though of course, one had to weigh in the balance also the loss of the Waymark Prize.

'Oh, no,' said Lady B. 'We got that. Haven't you heard? It went to Li Tao, for his work on number theory.'

'For the ABC conjecture?' exclaimed Imogen.

'Mathematics is a deeply mysterious subject,' said Lady B. 'What's the time? I must be back at my car at five o'clock, because I'm dining in Girton this evening. I never miss this one. It's the night of the year when the college MAs all dine without their gowns, in commemoration of all those women graduates who were denied the titles of their degrees in the past.'

'When were women let in?' asked Pamela.

'Not fully till 1948. And I often wonder what became of them all – learned ladies, dispersed in the world trying to get teaching jobs in competition with certificated graduates from London and Oxford . . . Perhaps most of them just got married and disappeared into remote places. Anyway, I like going gownless in their memory.'

Imogen drove home, and went straight to the phone.

'How's your leg?' asked Mrs Evans. 'And those bites?'

'I'm fine,' said Imogen. 'Back to normal. I've been thinking about Granny Vi. Did she have university education, do you know?'

'Grandad always said she was too clever by half. But I don't know about educated. Why don't you ask her?'

'*Ask* her? But I thought . . . surely someone told me she had gone . . .'

'Gone to England, not to meet her maker. She's in a nursing home in Shrewsbury. Very pretty gardens, and the matron so kind . . .'

'But however old is she?'

'Ninety-four in August. She can't get about without a zimmer frame, only with a wheelchair. But she's as sharp as needles to talk to . . .'

Imogen got the telephone number of the home, and arranged to visit Granny Vi. And since her leg still ached if she drove a long distance, she extracted Fran from the task of writing the great life, and took her along for a weekend break.

The home to which Granny Vi had retreated was a large Edwardian mock-Tudor mansion, on the outskirts of the town. Imogen and Fran found a bed-and-breakfast place, booked in for the night, had a pub lunch, and went on their visit. Mrs Evans senior was sitting sunning herself in a conservatory overlooking the garden, her eyes shut, her head tilted into the light. A patchwork square lay neglected in her

176

lap. She was wearing a rather squashed straw hat over her spiky grey hair, but the brim did not shade her face when she looked upwards at that angle. The matron pointed her out to her visitors, and they approached. Fran's shadow fell across the wrinkled and freckled face of the old lady, and she opened her eyes at once.

'Mrs Evans?' said Imogen. 'We've come to see you.'

'Am I Mrs Evans?' she said, surprisingly, squinting up at them against the light, with bright brown eyes. 'I suppose I am. Miss Violet Margery Passmore is who I am *really*, you know.'

'Didn't you get used to being Mrs Evans, in all that time in Wales?' said Imogen, smiling.

'Not really. Of course, young women now don't change their names when they marry, so I understand. Cheeky monkeys! But if a married woman can keep her old name, I think I might be allowed to have my old one back, don't you?'

'Of course; whyever not?' said Fran. 'I'm certainly aiming to hold on to mine.'

'And what is that, dear?'

'Frances Bullion.'

'Yes. A nice solid, twenty-two carat sort of name. But do I know you? You have probably come to see one of the other old ladies. There's quite a choice of old ladies here! But I'm sure I don't know anyone called Bullion.'

'No, you don't know me. But it is you we have come to see. I'm with Imogen here – Imogen Quy.'

'Oh, yes; my daughter-in-law told me you might come. You are very welcome, you know. One doesn't make many *new* acquaintances at my age. You'll be quite a thrill! Are you going to take me out to tea?'

'Certainly we are, if you would like that,' said Imogen. 'Can you manage the car, and steps and such?'

'Given time I can,' said Granny Vi. 'They do a very nice cream tea at the Stanhope Hotel.'

'The Stanhope Hotel it is, then!' said Fran.

Granny Vi hauled herself to her feet with the aid of her walking frame, and set off down the terrace at a steady pace. Fran picked up her needlework, and they followed.

It was quite all right for her to go out with friends, the matron said. Imogen didn't even have to declare herself as a nurse.

'Kidnapped!' cried Granny Vi, as Fran drove her out of the gates. 'Oh what fun! Spiffing!'

'But it wouldn't be if we had really kidnapped you,' said Fran.

'As long as I get my tea,' the old girl said. 'The buns in the home are always stale.'

It was a bit of a struggle for Granny Vi to get herself out of the car, and up the steps, and into the hotel. She was frail, and slow. But she gave Imogen the curious impression that she was *good* at being frail; quite practised and skilled at it. There was no mishap. The Stanhope produced an excellent tea, in a comfortable sunny lounge. Cucumber sandwiches, and scones, and Madeira cake, and a choice of Darjeeling or Earl Grey in a proper teapot, and porcelain plates and cups.

'None of those horrid little dangling paper bits attached to teabags, either,' Granny Vi pointed out. 'Just real, mashed tea. Lovely.'

'You're right, it is good,' said Imogen.

'Now my dear, I didn't get to ninety without realising that I don't get tea for nothing,' said Granny Vi. 'What do you two want of me?'

'Well, I am writing the life of a dead don, you see,' Fran told her. 'I am a biographer. What he's mostly famous for is inventing a pattern – this pattern.' Fran took a sheet of paper out of her bag and held it out to Granny Vi.

'I can't see too well these days,' Granny Vi said. 'But it looks familiar, I must say.'

'We think he didn't invent it; we think he saw a quilt that you had made,' said Imogen.

'Typical,' said Granny Vi. 'Bloody typical, if you'll pardon my French.'

'Typical of what, exactly?' Fran asked.

'Men. Dons. Just *hate* the achievements of women. Well, I must remember that times change. They did, thenadays. In my days.'

'We want you to tell us about the quilt,' Imogen said. 'When did you make it?'

'Can't remember exactly. The thing about a farm, you know, is that one year is much like another. It might have been in 1935. Some time before the war.'

'It's brilliant,' said Fran. 'And it is a non-periodic pattern, isn't it? Where did you learn the maths?'

'Cambridge,' said Granny Vi. 'Disgusting place. In my time, that is.'

'What do you mean?' asked Fran. 'It's rather good, now.'

But when Granny Vi had been Violet Margery Passmore, reading mathematics at Newnham College, women had still been outsiders.

She had come up to Cambridge without having realised that the battle was still raging there; women had long been able to take degrees at London, Oxford, Durham. She had thought of the struggle for access to education as a battle already won; just a little tidying up still needed ... She had assumed that by the time she took her degree – three years away, and three years seemed for ever to a young woman – it would all be sorted out. She turned out to be good; had been expected by her tutors to emulate the famous Philippa Fawcett, she who had come above the senior wrangler in the lists.

And then she found Cambridge once again voting to deny her her degree. Worse; she had been terrified. When the result of the vote was announced, a mob of male students charged from the Senate House and battered at the gates of her Newnham, trying to break in, and shouting obscenities at the young women within. Violet Passmore had been in the town visiting a friend. When she returned to the college and saw the uproar, she had boldly, and unwisely, tried to push her way through the howling crowd of men, to get round to the back gate, and get in. She had been pushed, and pulled, and man-handled, and finally had her nose broken by a punch to the face.

A policeman had rescued her, and bundled her unceremoniously through a downstairs window, flung open by one of the tutors. She had landed, blood streaming down her face, on the floor inside. And it was too much for her. Too much, she declared, all these long years later, for any self-respecting woman. To go through that sort of ordeal to take an exam that would not even confer a proper degree? She had left Cambridge in disgust without taking finals, and married a young farmer with land in Wales.

Being a farmer's wife offered a good life, but short on mathematics. The farm accounts didn't challenge Mrs Evans much. But at least Mr Evans respected her intelligence, and he never punched her in the face. He even purported to like the slight kink left by the healed break in her nose.

'He was a lovely man,' Granny Vi said, fondly.

And it was amusing to work out patterns for quilts. She had loved patchwork ever since Gwenny's mother at the farm nearby first showed her how to make them. Only now it was so hard – her eyesight was failing.

Fran offered indignation and admiration in lavish amounts. Granny Vi ate doggedly, stuffing herself with tea till all the plates were empty. Then they took her for a little drive around – 'I don't get out much, these days,' she had told them. And then they took her home.

'Don't you ever regret that degree, and. that lost life as a mathematics scholar?' Imogen asked, as they were just about to take their leave.

'No point in regrets. Regrets kill you at my age,' said Granny Vi briskly. 'And anger is wasted on such duff-heads. I soon saw that.'

'Can we do anything for you, before we go?' asked Fran.

'Yes please; will you thread a dozen needles for me? That will keep me going till tomorrow.'

Imogen and Fran set about threading every needle in Granny Vi's needlecase with white thread. It had to be white, these days, otherwise she couldn't see her own stitches.

'So you see, Fran,' said Imogen that evening, as they settled down to play travel Scrabble in their twin-bedded, over-cosily furnished room, 'it *was* from a colleague that your Gideon stole his work.'

'Does it matter whether it was from a colleague or not?' said Fran. 'I wonder. I've drawn X – you go first.'

'You'll never guess who I've just been talking to,' said Fran to Imogen a few days after their return home.

'You'll have to tell me then, if you want me to know,' said Imogen absently. She was browsing in a quilters' guild catalogue, looking for fabric samples.

'Ian Goliard.'

'Really? How? Where? What's he like?'

'Leo introduced me. In college this morning. He's, well – ineffable.'

'Tell me more.'

'Very long and weedy. Very posh and dreamy. Congratulating himself mightily on escaping all the unpleasantness.' Fran put on an affected voice. '"But my dehah! How perfectly frightful for you! I don't know *what* I would have done in your place . . ." That sort of thing.'

'Well, I suppose it should be a great relief that he's still alive. We shouldn't expect him to be nice as well,' said Imogen.

'Oh, he's perfectly nice. And hugely useful. He has kept loads of letters – though admittedly most of them are to rather than from the great Gideon.'

'*To* the great Gideon? But how has he got them if he sent them?'

'He's a bit of a card. And not very modest; he obviously kept copies to assist future biographers. His own biographers, that is. I'm afraid

I let slip that I hadn't read him – Goliard that is. He's a poet, did you know? Anyway quick as a flash he produced this –' Fran waved a thin pamphlet on crunchy paper – 'Poems; privately printed – and autographed it for me before I could ask him to!'

'Are they any good?' asked Imogen.

'Look and see. You tell me,' said Fran, tossing the pamphlet on the table. Imogen began to read:

> 'The river parts and joins again
> Around the islets of Coe Fen,
> Where come and go our learned men.
> Down from the fields of Grantchester,
> Where pub-bound scholars still confer,
> It brims and roars across the weir . . .
> So green is never another stream,
> Flowing these ancient lawns between
> Its surface bright, its depths unseen
> The willows lean with casual grace,
> Their fronds caress the water's face
> Their greenness glorifies the place . . .'

So great was the contrast between the quality of the words and the beauty of the hand-laid paper it was hard to avoid the sense that a fine empty book had been disfigured by printing this stuff in it.

'Ugh!' said Imogen, putting it down again.

'It's a bit, well – derivative, don't you think?' said Fran, grinning. 'Sounds as though every line was lifted from another poem that one has certainly seen somewhere, but can't quite remember. *Borrowing* must have been a habit in that lot of people!'

Naturally Imogen had told Lady Buckmote all about Granny Vi. And Sir William Buckmote, St Agatha's respected and influential head of house, got to hear about her too. And that is how it happened that on a glorious sunny day in early summer a very frail old lady was wheeled into the Senate House, among flocks of gowned and capped and fancy-dressed academic eminences, to receive an honorary degree. A reception for her in Newnham was to follow, at which, she had confided to Imogen, she intended to make a gift to her old college of the mathematical quilt; and at her earnest request she was pushed there in her wheelchair, so that she could once again cross the river at Garret Hostel Bridge, and admire what must be one of the loveliest vistas in Europe.

Quite a little bevy of people paused at the apex of the bridge, to admire the often recollected view. A light breeze swung the pendulant willow fronds, and billowed in the sleeves of the gowns, and fluttered the downy white hair of the old lady, who stared so eagerly at the arcadian vista of bridges and gardens. The bright new academic gown she was wearing seemed far too big for her, and emphasised her tiny bent frame.

'You know,' she said, addressing nobody in particular. 'I loved this place so much. And I always felt excluded, I never felt I belonged. But I do now – very much so!'

The green-brown river below them, swirling and sparkling, made endlessly recurring, but never precisely repeating, patterns of reflected light.

19047951R00113

Made in the USA
Lexington, KY
05 December 2012